THE
ORCHARD BOOK OF

Classic

Shakespeare

Stories

For Keith, Pat and Terry
A.M.

To Heather Rogers,
for all the happy hours
A.B.

In the same series
THE ORCHARD BOOK OF STORIES FROM THE BALLET
Retold by Geraldine McCaughrean
Illustrated by Angela Barrett

THE ORCHARD BOOK OF GREEK MYTHS
Retold by Geraldine McCaughrean
Illustrated by Emma Chichester Clark

THE ORCHARD BOOK OF GREEK GODS AND GODDESSES
Retold by Geraldine McCaughrean
Illustrated by Emma Chichester Clark

THE ORCHARD BOOK OF ROMAN MYTHS
Retold by Geraldine McCaughrean
Illustrated by Emma Chichester Clark

ORCHARD BOOKS
338 Euston Road, London NW1 3BH
Orchard Books Australia
Level 17/207 Kent Street, Sydney, NSW 2000
First published in 2001 by Orchard Books
This edition published in 2014
ISBN 978 1 40833 266 5
Text © Andrew Matthews 2001
Illustrations © Angela Barrett 2001
The rights of Andrew Matthews to be identified as the author and Angela Barrett to be
identified as the illustrator of this work have been asserted by them in accordance with
the Copyright, Designs and Patents Act, 1988.
A CIP catalogue record for this book is available from the British Library.
2 4 6 8 10 9 7 5 3 1
Printed in China
Orchard Books is a division of Hachette Children's Books, an Hachette UK company.
www.hachette.co.uk

THE
ORCHARD BOOK OF
Classic
Shakespeare
Stories

RETOLD BY
ANDREW MATTHEWS

ILLUSTRATED BY
ANGELA BARRETT

ORCHARD

CONTENTS

FOREWORD

There is a magic about the theatre. When the lights dim and the audience falls silent, the atmosphere becomes expectant, rather like the air just before a storm. Then the curtains rise and the actors start to speak their lines. Almost at once, the audience forgets about props, scenery and costumes. The actors are the characters they portray and the stage turns into a castle, a battlefield, a wood at midnight – wherever the play is set – and what happens becomes as real as real life itself.

Shakespeare understood the magic of theatre so well that today, almost four hundred years after his death, his plays still cast a spell over the thousands of people who go to see them.

Like all the playwrights of his day, Shakespeare borrowed his plots from stories that were popular at the time. *King Henry the Fifth* and *Macbeth* were taken from the writings of the historian Raphael Holinshed. *A Midsummer Night's Dream* was based on stories by Geoffrey Chaucer and the Latin writers Ovid and

Apuleius. *Romeo and Juliet* was a well-known tale in Italy and France, and Shakespeare probably came to know it through a play by Arthur Brooke, *The Tragical History of Romeus and Juliet*. Sir Thomas North translated the works of the Roman historian Plutarch into English, which Shakespeare must have read before writing *Antony and Cleopatra*. A Frenchman, Bellefrost, wrote a famous collection of stories which included *Hamlet* and *Twelfth Night*. Only *The Tempest* seems to have been written by Shakespeare himself.

But Shakespeare did more than just copy the stories, he shaped them into spellbinding plays and gave his actors wonderful lines to speak. Though his work has been carefully studied by great scholars, Shakespeare did not intend people to sit down and read his plays – they were meant to be acted in the theatre in front of an audience; only there can their magic truly happen.

A MIDSUMMER NIGHT'S DREAM

Love and magic in
the woods of Ancient Athens

CAST LIST

HERMIA in love with Lysander

HELENA friend to Hermia, in love with Demetrius

OBERON King of the Fairies

TITANIA Queen of the Fairies

PUCK an elf

DEMETRIUS betrothed to Hermia

LYSANDER in love with Hermia

BOTTOM a weaver

THE SCENE
In and around Athens, Ancient Greece

Ay me, for aught that I could ever read,

Could ever hear by tale or history,

The course of true love never did run smooth,

LYSANDER; ACT ONE, SCENE ONE

When the path of true love runs smoothly, the world seems a wonderful place – all bright skies and smiling faces. Unfortunately, true love has a habit of wandering off the path and getting lost, and when that happens people's lives get lost too, in a tangle of misery.

Take the love of Duke Theseus of Athens and Hippolyta, Queen of the Amazons, for instance. They were to be married, and their happiness spread through the whole of Athens. People had decorated their houses with flowers, and left lamps burning in their windows at night, so that the streets twinkled like a city of stars. Everybody was joyful and excited as they prepared to celebrate the Duke's wedding day.

Well, almost everybody…

+   +   +

On the day before the royal wedding, two friends met by chance in the market square: golden-haired Hermia, and black-haired Helena, both beautiful and both with secrets that made their hearts ache.

For a while, the two friends chatted about nothing in particular. Then Helena noticed a look in Hermia's deep blue eyes that made her ask, "Is everything all right, Hermia?"

Hermia looked so sad and serious. "I am to marry Demetrius tomorrow," she replied.

"Demetrius!" said Helena softly. Now her heart was aching worse than ever. Night after night she had cried herself to sleep, whispering Demetrius's name, knowing that her love for him was hopeless. Many

years ago the families of Hermia and Demetrius had agreed that, when they were of age, their daughter and son should marry. "You must be the happiest young woman in Athens!" sighed Helena.

"I've never been so miserable in my life!" Hermia declared. "You see, I don't love Demetrius."

"You don't?" cried Helena, amazed.

"I'm in love with Lysander," Hermia confessed, and she began to describe all the things that made Lysander so wonderful.

Helena thought about Lysander, with his curly brown hair and broad smile. He was *quite* handsome, she supposed, but he didn't have Demetrius's dark, brooding good looks. Why on earth did Hermia find him so attractive?

"Of course, I told my father that I didn't wish to marry Demetrius," Hermia said, "and he went straight to him to explain – but you know how stubborn Demetrius can be. He lost his temper and said it didn't matter who I loved, our marriage had been arranged and it must go ahead, no matter what. His stupid pride's been hurt, that's all – he doesn't love me a bit."

"Then who does he love?" Helena enquired eagerly.

"No one, except for himself," said Hermia. "I *can't* marry someone I don't love, and I know it will cause a scandal, but Lysander and I are going to run away together!"

"*When?*" Helena asked.

"Tonight," Hermia told her. "I'm meeting him at midnight in the wood outside the city walls. We plan to travel through the night, and in the morning we'll find a little temple where we can be married. Oh, Helena, it will be so *romantic*! Please say that you're happy for me!"

"Of course I am," said Helena. "I'm overjoyed."

And she was overjoyed – for herself. 'At last, this is my chance!' she

thought. 'If I visit Demetrius tonight and tell him that Hermia and Lysander have gone off together, he'll forget about his pride...and then…when I tell him how I feel about him, he'll be so flattered, he'll fall in love with me. Love always finds a way!'

Which is true, but love doesn't always find the way that people expect, as Helena was about to find out. For it was not only in the human world that love was causing unhappiness; although Helena and Hermia did not know it, two different worlds would meet in the wood outside Athens that night, and the result would be chaos.

✦   ✦   ✦

Oberon, King of the Fairies, was a creature of darkness and shadows, while his wife, Queen Titania, was moonlight and silver. The two loved each other dearly, but they had quarrelled bitterly. Titania had taken a little orphan boy as a page, and made such a fuss of the lad that Oberon had become very jealous. He wanted the page for himself.

That midsummer's night, in a clearing in the wood, Titania was singing to her page, while fairy servants fluttered around her like glittering moths.

When Oberon appeared, Titania's silvery eyes darkened. "Fairies, let us leave this place at once!" she said haughtily.

"Wait, Titania!" snapped Oberon. "This quarrel of ours has gone on long enough. You say I have no reason to be jealous of the boy – very well, prove it! Give him to me!"

"Not for all your fairy kingdom!" hissed Titania. She raised her left hand, and sent a ball of blue fire roaring across the glade, straight at Oberon's head.

Oberon spoke a word of magic, and the fire turned to water that burst over him, drenching his clothes. By the time he had rubbed the water from his eyes, the glade was empty and Oberon was alone. "I'll make you sorry for this, Titania!" he vowed. Then, lifting his dripping head, he called out, "Puck? Come to me, now!"

A breeze sighed in the branches, as an elf dropped out of the air and landed at Oberon's feet. The elf was dressed in leaves that had been sewn together. His hair was tangled, his skin as brown as chestnuts, and when he smiled, his white teeth flashed mischievously. "Command me,

master!" Puck said.

"I mean to teach the Queen a lesson," said Oberon. "Go, search the Earth and fetch me the flower called Love in Idleness."

"I will fly faster than a falling star!" said Puck, and with that he had vanished.

A cruel smile played on Oberon's lips. "When Titania is asleep, I will drop the juice of the flower in her eyes," he said to himself. "Its magic will make her fall in love with the first living thing she sees when she wakes – perhaps a toad, or even a spider! She will make herself seem so ridiculous, that she will beg me to break the spell, and I will…after she's given me the page!"

This plan pleased Oberon so much that he began to laugh – but his laugh was cut short when he heard human voices approaching. With a wave of his fingers, Oberon made himself vanish among the shadows.

+   +   +

Demetrius, out searching for Hermia, halted in the middle of the glade, while he considered which path to take. This gave Helena a chance to catch up with him. "Wait for me, Demetrius!" she pleaded.

Demetrius scowled at her. "For the last time, Helena, go home!" he shouted angrily. "I can find Lysander and Hermia without your help."

"But you don't understand!" Helena exclaimed. "I love you! I've always loved you!"

She tried to put her arms around Demetrius, but he ducked away. "Well I don't love you!" he said roughly. "So go away and leave me alone!" And he ran off through the moonlight.

"Oh, Demetrius!" sobbed Helena, running after him. "I would follow you through fire, just to be near you!"

+   +   +

When the glade was once more still and silent, Oberon came out of the darkness. His face was thoughtful. "I must help that lovely maiden!" he whispered. "I know how cruel it is to love someone whose heart is so cold."

A wind brushed the Fairy King's cheek, and there stood Puck, holding a sprig of glimmering white flowers.

"Take two blossoms and search the woods for a young human couple," Oberon said to him. "Squeeze the juice of the petals into the young man's eyes, but do it when you are sure that the maiden will be the first thing he sees."

"At once, master!" Puck said with a bow, and then he was gone.

Then Oberon went to find Titania. He found her sleeping alone on a bank of violets, and the air was heavy with their sweet perfume. As he dropped juice from the magic flowers on to Titania's eyelids, Oberon murmured:

"What you see when you awake,
Do it for your true love take!"

+ + +

At that very moment, in another part of the wood, Puck was putting magic juice into the eyes of a young man he had found sleeping next to a young woman at the foot of a pine tree.

"When he wakes and sees her, his love for her will drive him mad!" Puck giggled, and he leapt into the air, like a grasshopper in a summer meadow.

But, as bad luck would have it, Puck had found the wrong couple. Those sleeping under the tree were Lysander and Hermia, who had got lost in the wood and exhausted themselves trying to find the way out.

And as bad luck would also have it, a few seconds after Puck had left them, Helena wandered by, searching for Demetrius. Blinded by tears, Helena did not notice Lysander and Hermia until she stumbled over Lysander's legs. He woke, saw her, and his eyes bulged like a frog's as the magic went to work.

"Lysander?" gasped Helena. "What are you doing here? I mean, you mustn't be here! Get away quickly! Demetrius is looking for you, and if he finds you…" Her voice trailed off – there was a strange look about Lysander, and it made her feel uncomfortable. "Why are you staring at me like that?" she asked.

"Because at last I have found my own true love," said Lysander. "Helena, can't you see how much I love you?"

Helena stepped back, laughing nervously. "Don't be silly, Lysander!" she said. "You love Hermia…don't you?"

"Hermia, who is she?" scoffed Lysander, scrambling to his feet. "How could I love anyone but you, with your eyes like stars, your hair as black

as ravens' wings, and your skin as soft as…?"

"That's quite enough of that!" said Helena. "This is some sort of midsummer madness!"

"Madness? Yes, I'm mad!" said Lysander. "Mad with love for you! Come to my arms, and cool the fires of my passion with your kisses!"

He moved towards Helena, but she turned and fled. Lysander followed her, shouting, "There's no escape from love, Helena! This was meant to be!"

Their loud voices and pounding footsteps woke Hermia. "Lysander, where are you?" she muttered sleepily. "Don't wander off on your own, my love. You might be eaten by a lion, or a bear…" The very thought made her wide awake, and she sat up. "Or I might be eaten, come to that!" she said with a shudder. "I'm coming to find you, Lysander, so we can be eaten together!"

+   +   +

Not five paces from the bank of violets where Titania lay asleep, a group of Athenians had gathered in secret to rehearse a play that they meant to perform for Duke Theseus after his wedding. One of the actors, a weaver called Bottom, was behind a tree, waiting to appear when he heard his cue. "I'll show them how it's done!" Bottom said to himself. "When the Duke sees what a fine actor I am, he'll give me a purse of gold, or my name's not Nick Bottom!"

He glanced up, and saw a strange orange light circling the tree. "Now what's that, I wonder?" he muttered. "A firefly perhaps?"

It was Puck. He had noticed the actors as he flew by on his way back to Oberon, and had seen a chance to make mischief. "Behold, the Queen's new love!" he said. Magic sparks showered down from his fingertips on to the weaver.

Immediately Bottom's face began to sprout hair, and his nose and ears grew longer and longer. His body was unchanged, so Bottom had no idea that anything was wrong, until he heard his cue and stepped out from behind a tree.

Bottom had meant his entrance to be dramatic, and it certainly was. The other actors took one look at the donkey-headed monster coming towards them, and raced away screaming and shouting.

"What's the matter with them?" said Bottom, scratching his chin. "My word, my beard has grown quickly today! I'll need a good shave before the performance tomorrow!" He paced this way and that, puzzling out why his friends had left in such a hurry. "O-o-h! I see-haw, hee-haw!" he said at last. "They're trying to frighten me by leaving me alone in the wood in the dark! Well it won't work! It takes more than that to frighten a man like me-haw, hee-haw!"

And to prove how brave he was, Bottom began to sing. His voice was part human, part donkey and it sounded like the squealing of rusty hinges. It woke Queen Titania from her sleep on the bank of violets. "Do I hear an angel singing?" she said, and raised herself on one elbow and gazed at Bottom. "Adorable human, I have fallen wildly in love with you!" she told him.

"Really?" said Bottom, not the least alarmed by the sudden appearance of the Fairy Queen. He was sure it was all part of the trick his friends were playing.

"Sit beside me, so I can stroke your long, silky ears!" Titania purred.

"My servants will bring you anything you desire."

"I wouldn't say no to some supper," said Bottom. "Nothing fancy – a bale of hay or a bag of oats would suit me fine!"

From up above came the sound of Puck's laughter, like the pealing of tiny bells.

✦   ✦   ✦

Oberon's laughter set every owl in the wood hooting. "My proud Queen, in love with a donkey?" he cried. "Well done, Puck! Titania will think twice before she defies me again! But what of the humans?"

"I did as you commanded, master," said Puck. "I found them…"

A voice made him turn his head, and he saw Demetrius stamping along the path, dragging Hermia by the arm.

"That is the fellow!" said Oberon. "But who is that with him?"

"He is not the one I cast the spell on!" Puck yelped.

"Quickly," said Oberon. "Make yourself invisible before they see us!"

✦   ✦   ✦

Hermia was thoroughly miserable. Everything had gone wrong: she had found Demetrius instead of Lysander, and Demetrius was in such a foul temper that she feared the worst. "Oh, where is Lysander?" she wailed. "You've killed him, haven't you, you brute?"

With a weary groan, Demetrius let Hermia go and slumped to the ground.

"I haven't touched your precious Lysander!" he yawned. "Now stop

whining and get some sleep. When it's light, we'll find our way out of this accursed wood."

"I won't rest until I find Lysander!" Hermia said defiantly.

"Just as you wish," said Demetrius. "I'm too tired to argue any more."

He lay back among the ferns and closed his eyes. He heard Hermia walking away, and then he fell into a deep sleep.

Moonlight shifted and shivered as Oberon and Puck reappeared. "This is the man," said Oberon, peering down at Demetrius. "Search the wood for a black-haired maiden, and bring her here. When she is close by I will put magic juice in his eyes and wake him."

"Yes, master! But tell me, is human love always so complicated?" Puck asked curiously.

"Just do as I have commanded!" snapped Oberon.

✦   ✦   ✦

Helena was still running, with Lysander just a few steps behind her. So many bewildering things had happened to her, that when an orange light appeared above the path in front of her, she was not surprised – in fact, a curious idea suddenly popped into her mind – Puck's magic had put it there. Helena became convinced that if she followed the light, it would lead her back to Athens, and sanity. Over streams and through clearings the light led her, until at last she came to a deep thicket of ferns, where she paused for breath.

"Helena, marry me!" she heard Lysander shout.

"I don't want you!" she shouted back. "I want Demetrius!"

"And here I am, my love!" said Demetrius, springing up out of the ferns nearby, his eyes glowing with magic. "Hold me, let me melt in your sweetness!"

Helena did not bother to wonder why Demetrius had changed his mind: her dreams had come true, and she was about to rush into his arms when Lysander ran between them.

"Keep away from her, Demetrius!" Lysander said hotly. "Helena is mine!"

"Lysander...is that you?" called a voice, and Hermia came stumbling out of the bushes. Brambles had torn the hem of her dress, and there were leaves and twigs stuck in her hair. "Thank the gods you're safe!" she said, weeping for joy. "Why did you leave me, my only love?"

"Because I can't bear the sight of you!" said Lysander. "I want to marry Helena."

"So do I!" Demetrius exclaimed. "And since she can't marry both of us, we'll have to settle the matter, man to man!"

He pushed Lysander's chest, knocking him backwards, then Lysander pushed Demetrius.

Hermia stared at Helena, her eyes blazing. "You witch! You've stolen my Lysander!" she screeched.

"I haven't stolen anybody!" Helena replied angrily. "This is all some cruel trick, isn't it? The three of you plotted together to make a fool of me – and I thought you were my friend!"

"Our friendship ended when you took Lysander away from me!" snarled Hermia.

And there might have been a serious fight, if Oberon had not cast a sleeping spell on all four of them. They dropped to the ground like ripe apples, Hermia falling close to Lysander and Helena collapsing at Demetrius's side.

Oberon and Puck appeared magically beside them.

"Smear their eyes with fairy juice!" said Oberon. "This knot of lovers will unravel when they wake."

As Puck hurried about his task, the air was filled with the singing of fairy voices. "The Queen!" Puck muttered in alarm. "The Queen is coming!"

✦   ✦   ✦

Titania did not notice Puck and Oberon, or the sleeping lovers. She could see nothing but Bottom, whose jaws were stretched open in a wide yawn. "Are you weary, dearest one?" she asked him tenderly. "Rest with me on these soft ferns."

"I feel a powerful sleep coming over me-haw, hee-haw!" said Bottom.

"Fairies, leave us!" ordered Titania.

The fairies flew away, leaving bright trails in the air. Titania cradled Bottom's head in her lap, and they both dozed.

Oberon and Puck crept close. Puck began to grin, but he stopped when he saw the sorrow in his master's eyes.

"There is no laughter in this!" Oberon sighed. "How I long for Titania to smile at me, as she smiled at this creature, and to feel her soft arms around me as I sleep! Break the spell on the human, Puck, while I deal with the Queen."

Oberon moved his hands, weaving shadows into magic as he chanted:

"Be the way you used to be,
See the way you used to see,
Wake, my Queen, and come to me!"

Titania opened her eyes, and when she saw Oberon she flew straight into his arms. "I am so glad that you are here, my love!" she said. "I had the strangest dream! I dreamed that I had fallen in love with a…"

"We will never quarrel again," Oberon promised. "Keep your page – have fifty pages if you wish! What does it matter, as long as we are together?"

Puck saw that the sky was getting lighter. "It's almost dawn, master!" he warned.

"Then we must leave!" said Oberon, and he, Titania and Puck faded into the pale morning light.

When the sun rose, its light woke Demetrius and Helena, who fell in love at first sight, then Lysander and Hermia, who fell in love all over again. There was much smiling, sighing and kissing, and soon Demetrius said, "Today is Duke Theseus's wedding day, as well as mine and Helena's. Come, my friends, the priest can marry us all at the same ceremony!"

And the lovers hurried off towards Athens, laughing every step of the way, the paths of their true love running smoothly at last.

+ + +

And as for Bottom, he woke some time later and clambered stiffly to his feet. "I thought I was…!" He mumbled. "I thought I had…!" Anxiously, he felt his face and ears, and then sighed with relief. "What a midsummer night's dream!" he exclaimed. "I'll write a poem about it, and read it to Duke Theseus and his bride, and the Duke will say: 'Well done, noble Bottom! Here's some gold for you!'"

And he stumbled away through the ferns, making up lines of poetry and reciting them out loud as he went.

The eye of man hath not heard, the ear of man hath not seen, man's hand is not able to taste, his tongue to conceive, nor his heart to report what my dream was.
BOTTOM; ACT FOUR, SCENE ONE

KING HENRY THE FIFTH

How a boy king won a mighty battle

CAST LIST

KING HENRY THE FIFTH

DUKE OF EXETER uncle to the King

A French ambassador

EARL OF CAMBRIDGE a conspirator against the King

A French messenger

MICHAEL WILLIAMS a soldier in the King's army

THE SCENE
England and France
in the fifteenth century

I see you stand like greyhounds in the slips,

Straining upon the start. The game's afoot.

Follow your spirit, and upon this charge

Cry, 'God for Harry! England and Saint George!'

KING HENRY: ACT THREE, SCENE ONE

Hardly anyone called the new King 'Henry'. When they talked about him they said 'Hal' or 'Harry', or used one of his other nicknames. Everyone knew what a wild and rebellious teenager the young prince had been. He had spent more time with rascally old Sir John Falstaff, learning how to drink and gamble than he had with his royal father. Now the reckless young Harry was King, but no one knew what sort of king he would be. Some thought he would be a disaster, others said that only time would tell, but all were aware that the young King faced a difficult time as the new English monarch.

England and France had been at war for twenty-five years, and though the two countries had agreed a truce, the truce was an uneasy one. A weak English king who didn't have the support of his people might give the French just the chance they wanted to carry out a successful invasion...

✦   ✦   ✦

One morning, not long after Henry's coronation, the nobles of the High Council were gathered together in the Reception Chamber of the King's palace in London. Among them was the Duke of Exeter, the King's uncle. He knew that Henry was now about to face his most challenging test. 'How young and lonely he looks on that great throne,' Exeter thought. 'He has his mother's dark hair and soft eyes – but does he have any of his father's courage, I wonder?'

His question was soon answered, for just then the doors of the great chamber opened and an ambassador from the Dauphin, the Crown Prince of France, entered. The ambassador was a perfumed dandy with his curled beard, and the clothes he wore were as brightly-coloured as a peacock's feathers. Behind him, two guards carried a large wooden chest which they set down on the floor.

The ambassador gave an elaborate bow. "Your Highness," he said, in a voice as smooth as honey. "My master, the Dauphin, sends greetings."

"I want more than greetings," Henry replied coldly. "I asked King Charles to give me back the French lands that my father won from him. What is his answer?"

The ambassador ran his fingers through the curls of his beard and smirked. "The King is busy with important matters," he said. "His Majesty thought that since the Dauphin is closer to you in age, it would be better for him to deal with your request."

Henry felt a sting of anger at the ambassador's insolent tone, but he kept his voice calm. "And what is the Dauphin's message?" he asked.

"The Dauphin thinks you are a little too young to bother yourself with affairs of state," said the ambassador, gesturing towards the wooden chest. "So he has sent a present which he thinks will be more suitable than the right to French dukedoms."

The ambassador clicked his fingers and the guards opened the lid of the chest. It was filled with tennis balls. One of them fell out and rolled to the foot of Henry's throne.

The nobles glanced at each other anxiously. King Henry had been insulted and humiliated in front of all his courtiers. How would he respond?

Henry leaned over and picked up the ball at his feet. He bounced it once, and caught it in his right hand. "Tell the Dauphin that he has begun a game with me that he'll wish he had never started," he said. "His mockery will turn these tennis balls into cannon balls! The people of France may be laughing at the Dauphin's joke, but they'll weep before I'm finished!"

The ambassador's face went deathly pale. He bowed low and left the chamber. When the door closed behind him, the nobles began to talk among themselves. Most of them glanced admiringly at Henry, but the Earl of Cambridge scowled at the King. He raised his

voice above the hubbub in the chamber and said, "Your Majesty spoke hastily. You should have sought the advice of older and wiser men before plunging our country into war."

"An insult to me is an insult to the English people!" Henry snapped. "And besides, my lord Cambridge, I don't listen to the advice of traitors!"

Cambridge started as though someone had jabbed him with a knife point and his eyes bulged with fear.

"You thought that because of my youth, I could easily be deceived," Henry went on, "but I've found you out. You betrayed your country for French gold and worked as a spy for King Charles. Guards, take him to the Tower!"

The nobles stared in astonishment at the disclosure of Cambridge's treachery and at seeing the determination of their young King. He was wiser and stronger-minded than any of them had realised.

Men from all over the country answered the young King's call to war with France. Blacksmiths, wheelwrights, farm-workers, weavers and

clerks all left their homes and marched along the roads that led to Southampton. The younger men thought that war would be a kind of holiday and were eager for fame and glory; others, who had fought before and knew what battle was like, were grim-faced and silent.

At Southampton, the men began their training. Hour after hour and day after day they marched and drilled. At the archery butts men with longbows practised until their aim was true. Slowly, the raggle-taggle band of volunteers was transformed into an army. When all was ready, the English battle fleet set sail for the French port of Harfleur.

+   +   +

It took all day for Henry's men to cross the Channel and unload the ships. The men spent the night on the beach and were woken in the grey hours before dawn to sharpen their weapons and make ready their siege-ladders and battering-rams. On the skyline the walls of Harfleur looked like an ominous cloud.

When the sun rose, Henry rode out in front of his men on his dapple-grey war-horse, the early morning light glinting on his armour. "The English are a peaceful nation," he told the troops, "but when war comes, we can fight like tigers! Let the light of battle blaze in your eyes, to burn the courage of your enemies! Let your cry be: *God for Harry, England and St George!*"

Cannons roared like a gigantic wave breaking on the shore as the English army charged. By nightfall, Harfleur had fallen.

+   +   +

Henry was planning to advance to the port of Calais, which was already an English possession. The next morning a messenger arrived from King Charles.

"The King commands that you surrender to him and leave France while you still can!" the messenger declared scornfully. "He is camped at Agincourt with an army of fifty thousand. If you do not agree to his terms, he will advance and crush you!"

"Your Majesty!" the Duke of Exeter murmured. "We only have four thousand men. If the French attack us here, all will be lost!"

"Then we must go to them, Uncle," Henry said calmly. He turned to the messenger. "Tell King Charles that his army is in my way," he said. "I will march to Agincourt and, if he does not step aside, the earth will be red with French blood!"

+   +   +

And so the English advanced to Agincourt and set up camp facing the French, on a plain between two woods. When the French saw the size of the English army they whistled and jeered, beating their swords against their shields to make a great clamour.

But Henry shut his ears to their taunts and concentrated on positioning his forces. He discussed battle plans with his commanders late into the night and after they had left his tent, Henry tried to rest, but a whirlpool of doubts and fears swirled in his mind, and he could not sleep. Hoping to calm himself, he put on a hooded cloak

and went walking through the camp.

Men lay asleep, huddled around fires. The air was filled with the sound of snores, or voices shouting out in terror through nightmares. Across the plain glimmered the fires of the French camp, as numberless as the stars on a winter's night.

Henry was so deep in thought that he didn't notice a sentry on guard beside one camp fire until he almost walked on to the point of the man's spear.

"Who goes there?" barked the sentry.

"A friend," Henry replied.

"Who is your commander?"

"The Duke of Exeter."

The guard lowered his spear and pulled a face. "A fine soldier!" he grunted. "If he were leading the army instead of the King, we wouldn't be in this mess. I bet young Harry wishes he was back in London, tucked up safe in bed."

"The King wishes himself nowhere but here," said Henry.

The guard turned his head to spit into the fire. Light from the flames played across his broken nose and the long scar on his left cheek. "Kings!" he growled. "They do the arguing, but it's the likes of you and me who do the fighting and the dying!"

"Tomorrow the King will fight in the front line, alongside his men, you will see," said Henry.

"I'll wager a week's wages that he'll be at the back, with a fast horse ready for his escape!" the guard said bitterly.

"Very well," said Henry. "If we both survive, find me when the battle's over and we'll see who was right. What's your name?"

"Michael Williams," said the guard. "What's yours?"

"Harry le Roy," Henry said with a smile, then he passed on and disappeared into the darkness.

✦   ✦   ✦

In the early hours of the morning a thunderstorm broke. Rain fell mercilessly, drenching English and French alike and turning the plain into a sea of mud. The rain stopped just before dawn, but the sky was still filled with heavy black clouds.

The first line of the French army took the field, led by knights on horseback. The plumes on their helmets fluttered brightly against the dark sky, and their armour shone like silver. Behind them ran infantrymen in chain-mail coats, carrying blue shields painted with golden fleurs-de-lis.

Henry ordered his archers to stand ready and wait for his signal.

The French knights broke into a gallop. The hooves of the horses shook the ground, and spattered their riders with mud. The knights lowered their lances and screamed out a battle cry, but halfway to the English line, the French horses ran into boggy ground and the charge faltered. The knights pulled at their reins in panic, turning their horses to try and find firmer footing. The infantrymen caught up, and all was a surging chaos of whinnying horses and cursing men.

Henry drew his sword and swept it high above his head. "Fire!" he bellowed.

At his command, a thousand arrows left a thousand longbows and made a sound like the wind sighing through the boughs of a forest. A deadly hail struck the French, piercing armour, and flesh, and bone. Knights fell from their saddles and startled horses bolted, trampling anyone who stood in their way. Volley after volley of arrows whistled down, until the only movement on the battlefield came from the wounded as they attempted to crawl back to safety.

A second line of French troops charged. Once more the English archers stopped them. The French tried to retreat, but ran into their own third line as it came up behind them. It was then that Henry led his men in a charge. The two armies met with a clash like a clap of thunder.

The fighting lasted for two hours. The French soldiers, dismayed and confused, found that their commanders had been killed and there was no one to give them orders. They fought bravely, but the fury of the English attack proved too much for them, and at last they broke ranks and fled.

Seven thousand Frenchmen died at Agincourt, including many great noblemen. The English lost only a hundred men.

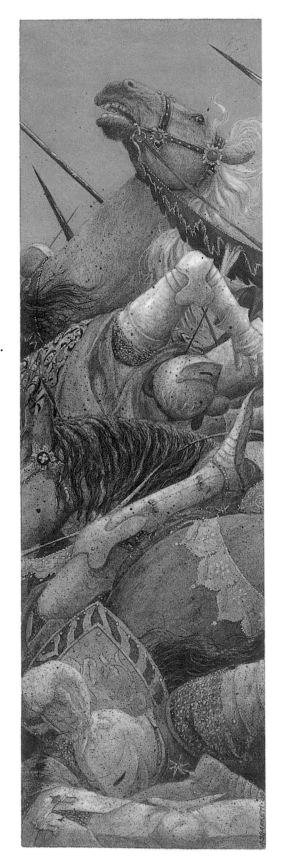

✦   ✦   ✦

That night, at sunset, a French messenger rode into the English camp carrying a white flag of truce. It was the same man who had come to Harfleur, but this time he was not haughty. His armour was dented and there was dirt and blood on his face. "King Charles begs for peace," he said humbly. "He will return all the lands that you claim and he asks you to accept the hand of his daughter, Princess Catherine, so that your two families may be united in peace forever."

"Tell the King that I accept," said Henry. "We will meet, and draw up a peace treaty."

That night, there were celebrations in the English camp and just before midnight, Henry slipped away from his commanders and went in search of Michael Williams. He found him at the same guard point as on the previous night.

When Williams saw Henry, he dropped to one knee. "Your Majesty," he mumbled. "I did not know who you were last night, but I recognised you today when you led the charge."

"So," said Henry, smiling. "I won the wager."

"I was a fool to speak the way I did last night!" said the sentry apologetically.

Henry put his hand on the man's shoulder and took a bag of gold coins from his belt. He handed it to the astonished guard. "Here," Henry said. "You spoke your mind last night. I hope that honest men will always speak to me as openly as you did."

+   +   +

So King Henry the Fifth won a famous victory – and more importantly, he won the hearts of all his subjects. Now they respected him as a ruler, but they also loved him because he understood the lives of ordinary people, and was always ready to listen to them. And he won more than his subjects' hearts, for when he met Catherine, the French princess, they fell in love at once – even though she could not speak English and his clumsy French made her laugh. With their marriage, the bitter war with France was ended in feasting and friendship.

This star of England. Fortune made his sword,
By which the world's best garden he achieved,
CHORUS; ACT FIVE, SCENE TWO

ROMEO AND JULIET

Love and misadventure in Verona

CAST LIST

JULIET daughter of Lord Capulet

ROMEO son of Lord Montague

TYBALT cousin to Juliet

LORD CAPULET

Nurse to Juliet

MERCUTIO friend to Romeo

BENVOLIO friend and cousin to Romeo

THE PRINCE OF VERONA

FRIAR LAWRENCE

A monk messenger to Friar Lawrence

THE SCENE
Verona in the fifteenth century

But soft, what light through yonder window breaks?

It is the east, and Juliet is the sun.

ROMEO; ACT TWO, SCENE ONE

On that warm summer's evening, the Capulet house was the brightest place in Verona. The walls of the ballroom were hung with silk tapestries, and candle-light from a dozen crystal chandeliers threw rainbows on to the heads of the masked dancers as they twirled through the music and laughter that filled the air.

On one side of the room, near a table laden with food and drink, stood a young girl, Juliet, the daughter of Lord and Lady Capulet. She had removed her mask and loosened her black hair so that it hung about her shoulders. Her face, flushed from the heat of the dance, was radiant and her beauty was obvious to all who looked at her. She seemed unaware that someone was watching her.

A few steps away, a young man stood gazing at her. He had never seen such loveliness before in his whole life.

'Surely I must be mistaken!' he thought. 'Surely, if I look a second time, I will find that her eyes are too close together, her nose too long or her mouth too wide!' Moving slowly towards her, as one in a trance, the young man lifted his mask so that he could see Juliet more clearly – and the more he gazed at her, the more perfect her face seemed.

Almost without thinking, Romeo pushed his way towards Juliet until he found himself standing at her side. Gently he took her hand.

Juliet turned her head, her soft brown eyes wide with surprise.

+   +   +

On the other side of the room, Tybalt, Lord Capulet's fiery young nephew, recognised the young man who was holding Juliet's hand, and strode angrily towards the door; but just as he was about to leave, his uncle caught him by the sleeve.

"Where are you going?" asked Lord Capulet.

"To fetch my rapier," Tybalt replied. "Lord Montague's son, Romeo, has dared to enter the house!"

"Leave him!" said Lord Capulet.

There was a terrible feud between the Capulets and the Montagues and the Prince of Verona had forbidden any more fighting between the two families, on pain of death.

Tybalt's face was ashen with rage. "But tomorrow, Romeo will boast to his friends about how he danced at the Capulets' ball and escaped without being noticed! He will make us look like fools!"

Lord Capulet put his hands on Tybalt's shoulders, forcing him to stop and listen. "I hate the Montagues as deeply as you do, Tybalt," he said. "Our two families have been at war with each other for as long as anyone can remember – but the Prince's word is law in this city, and there is to be no more fighting – you understand? Now, if you cannot keep your temper like a man, go to your room and sulk like a boy!"

Tybalt broke free from his uncle's grasp and glared across the room at Romeo. "You will pay for this one day, Montague!" he vowed softly. "I will make you pay!"

✦   ✦   ✦

Juliet glanced at the young man beside her, at his tightly-curled brown hair and startlingly grey eyes that were filled with shyness and wonder. His mouth was curved in a half-smile, and though it made her blush to look, Juliet found that she could not take her eyes from his face, or her hand from his.

"My lady," Romeo said, "if my hand has offended yours by holding it, please forgive me."

"My hand is not offended, sir," said Juliet, smiling at him, "and nor am I."

Some power that neither of them understood had drawn them together like a moth to a flame. They kissed and the ballroom, the musicians and dancers seemed to disappear, leaving them feeling as

though they were the only two people in the world.

When their lips parted, Romeo looked at Juliet and thought, 'All those other times, when I thought I was in love, I was like a child playing a game. This time I am truly in love – I wonder, could she possibly feel the same?'

Before he could ask, an elderly woman bustled up to them. "My lady," she said to Juliet, "your mother is asking for you."

Juliet frowned, shrugged helplessly at Romeo, then turned and walked away.

Romeo caught the old woman by the arm. "Do you know that lady?" he demanded.

"Why, sir, she is Juliet, Lord Capulet's daughter," said the woman. "I've been her nurse since she was a baby. And I know who you are, too, young man. Take my advice and leave this house, before there's trouble!"

✦   ✦   ✦

That night Juliet couldn't get to sleep. She could only think of Romeo. It was warm and the moonlight was shining on the trees in the orchard below. Juliet stepped out onto her balcony, but she was so troubled by what her nurse had told her, that she hardly noticed how lovely the orchard looked.

"How can I be in love with someone I ought to hate?" she sighed. "Oh, Romeo, why did you have to be a Montague? If you had been born with any other name, I could tell you how much I love you!"

Romeo stepped out of the shadows of the trees into the moonlight. "Call me your love," he said. "It is the only name I want!"

Juliet looked down from her balcony and gasped. "How did you get here? If anyone catches you, they will kill you!"

"I climbed the orchard wall," said Romeo. "I had to see you again! I loved you the moment I first saw you, and I wanted to know if you felt the same."

Juliet's face brightened with joy, then darkened into doubt. "How can I be sure of your love?" she said. "How can I be sure that you will not forget me as soon as tonight is over?"

Romeo looked up into Juliet's eyes and saw the way the moonlight shone in them. He knew he would never love anyone else. "Meet me at Friar Lawrence's chapel at noon tomorrow, and we shall be married!" he declared.

"Married?" laughed Juliet. "But we have only just met! And what will our parents say?"

"Do we need to meet more than once to know that our love is strong, and real?" said Romeo. "Must we live apart because of our families' hatred?"

A part of Juliet knew that for them to marry would be mad and impossible, but another part of her knew that if she sent Romeo away now, she might never see him again, and she wasn't sure she could bear that. "Yes!" she said. "Yes, I believe what we feel for each other is true! And yes, I'll meet you tomorrow at the chapel at noon!"

So, the next day Romeo and Juliet were married.

✦   ✦   ✦

The bell in the clock tower of the cathedral tolled twice. The main square of Verona sweltered in the hot sunshine and the air shimmered. Two young men were lounging beside a fountain and the taller of the two, Romeo's closest friend, Mercutio, dipped a handkerchief into the water and mopped his face. "Where is he?" he demanded tetchily. "He should have been here an hour ago!"

His companion, Romeo's cousin, Benvolio, smiled at Mercutio's impatience. "Some important business must have detained him," he said.

"A pair of pretty eyes, more like!" snorted Mercutio. But as he glanced across the square, he saw Romeo hurrying towards them. "At last!" Mercutio said sarcastically, "I was beginning to think that the Queen of the Fairies had carried you off in your sleep!"

"I have great news!" said Romeo. "But you must promise to keep it a secret!"

Mercutio looked curiously at his friend. "Oh?" he said.

"I am in love," said Romeo.

Benvolio laughed; Mercutio groaned and shook his head. "You are always in love!" he cried. "A girl only has to look at you sideways to make you fall for her."

"It's more than that this time," said Romeo. "I am in love with…"

"Romeo!" interrupted a harsh voice.

Romeo turned, and saw Tybalt with a group of sneering Capulets. Tybalt's right hand was resting on the hilt of his sword. "You were at my family's house last night," he said. "Now you must pay for your insolence. Draw your sword!"

Romeo's eyes flashed with anger, then grew calm. "I will not fight you, Tybalt," he said. "It would be like fighting one of my own family."

"Why, you milksop!" jeered Tybalt. "You're as cowardly as the rest of the Montagues."

"Romeo!" gasped Mercutio. "Are you going to stand and

do nothing while he insults
your family?"

"I must," said Romeo. "You don't
understand. I have no choice…"

"But I do!" snarled Mercutio.
His rapier flashed in the sunlight
as he drew it. "If you want a fight,
Tybalt, I'm your man!" he cried.

In a movement too fast to follow,
Tybalt brought out his sword and
the two young men began to fight
at a dazzling speed.

"Help me to stop them,
Benvolio!" pleaded Romeo. He
caught Mercutio from behind,
pinning his arms to his sides.
As he did so, Tybalt lunged
forward and drove the point of
his rapier through Mercutio's
heart, fatally wounding him.

"A plague on both your houses,"
he whispered with his dying breath.

When Romeo realised that his friend
was dead, rage surged through him
and his hatred of the Capulets brought
a bitter taste to his mouth. "Tybalt!"
he cried, drawing his rapier. "One of
us must join Mercutio in death!"

"Then let our swords decide who
it shall be!" Tybalt snarled.

Romeo hacked at Tybalt as though

Tybalt were a tree that he wanted to cut down. At first, the watching Capulets laughed at Romeo's clumsiness, but as Tybalt began to fall back towards the centre of the square, their laughter died. It was obvious that Tybalt was tiring and finding it difficult to defend himself.

At last, Romeo and Tybalt stood face to face, their swords locked together. Tybalt's left hand fumbled at his belt and he drew out a dagger. Romeo, seeing the danger, clamped his left hand around Tybalt's wrist, and they stumbled and struggled with each other.

Tybalt flicked out a foot, intending to trip Romeo, but instead he lost his own balance and the two enemies tumbled to the ground. Romeo fell on Tybalt's left hand, forcing the point of the dagger deep into Tybalt's chest. He felt Tybalt's dying breath warm against his cheek.

A voice called out, "Quick! The Prince's guards!" and the Capulets scattered.

Benvolio helped Romeo to his feet. "Come now, before it is too late," he said, but Romeo did not hear him. He stared at Tybalt's body, and the full realisation of what he had done fell on him like a weight. 'I have killed Juliet's cousin!' he thought. 'She cannot love a murderer! She will never forgive me! How could I have let myself be such a fool!'

He was still staring at Tybalt when the Prince's guards reached him.

✦ ✦ ✦

That night, the Prince of Verona passed judgement on Romeo. "The hatred of the Montagues and Capulets has cost two lives today," he said. "I want no more bloodshed. I will spare Romeo his life, but I banish him to the city of Mantua. He must leave tonight, and if he is ever found in Verona again, he will be put to death!"

✦ ✦ ✦

When Friar Lawrence heard the news of Romeo's banishment, he was deeply upset. He had already married Romeo and Juliet in secret, hoping that one day, their love would overcome the hatred between the Montagues and the Capulets – but it seemed that the hate had been too strong. After his evening meal, the Friar went to his chapel to say a prayer for the young lovers.

As he knelt in front of the altar, Friar Lawrence heard the sound of the chapel door opening, and footsteps racing up the aisle. He stood, turned and saw Juliet, who flung herself sobbing at his feet.

"Help me, Friar Lawrence!" she begged. "My father wants me to marry Count Paris, but I'd rather die than forsake Romeo."

"Do not despair, my child," Friar Lawrence urged. "Surely you can reason with your father?"

"I could not bring myself to tell him about Romeo," Juliet sobbed. "I pleaded Tybalt's death had made me too full of grief to think of marriage. But Father would not listen and the wedding is to take place tomorrow."

Friar Lawrence looked troubled. "There may be a way for you and Romeo to be together, my child, but it is dangerous," he said.

Friar Lawrence took a tiny bottle of blue liquid from the pouch at his belt. "Drink this tonight," he said, "and you will fall into a sleep as deep as death. Your parents will believe that you are dead and will put your body into the Capulet tomb – but in two days you will wake, alive and well."

"And Romeo?" said Juliet.

"I will send him a message explaining everything," said Friar Lawrence. "After you wake, you can go to Mantua in secret."

And so, on the morning of Juliet's wedding to Paris, the screams of her nurse woke the whole Capulet house. When the news of Juliet's death reached Benvolio, he rode straight to Mantua to Romeo. One of the travellers he passed on the way was a monk, who recognised him. "Lord Benvolio!" he called out as Benvolio approached. "I have a letter for your cousin Romeo from Friar Lawrence!"

"Out of my way!" Benvolio shouted back. "I have no time to stop!"

The monk watched as Benvolio galloped by on the road to Mantua. At that speed, the monk judged, Benvolio would be in the city before evening.

When Benvolio told Romeo that Juliet was dead, Romeo's heart broke and for hours he lay sobbing on his bed, while outside day turned into night. During that time, Benvolio stayed at Romeo's side, but he had no idea how to comfort his grief-stricken friend.

It was almost midnight before Romeo grew calm enough to speak. He sat up and wiped away his tears with the back of his hand.

"I must go to her," he said.

"But the Prince has banished you!" Benvolio reminded him. "If you are seen on the streets of Verona, it will mean your death."

"I am not afraid of death," said Romeo. "Without Juliet, my life means nothing. Go wake the grooms, and tell them to saddle my horse."

When Benvolio had left him alone, Romeo searched through the wooden chest at the foot of his bed until he found a green glass bottle that contained a clear liquid. "I shall drink this poison, and die at Juliet's side!" he vowed.

Romeo left Mantua at daybreak, refusing to let Benvolio accompany him. Once out of the city, he travelled along winding country tracks so that he could approach Verona without being seen. It was night when he arrived and with the hood of his cloak drawn up to hide his face, he slipped in unrecognised through the city walls at the main gate.

He went straight to the Capulet tomb, and it was almost as if someone had expected him, for the door was unlocked, and the interior was lit by a burning torch.

Romeo looked around, saw Tybalt's body, pale as candle wax – then Juliet, laid out on a marble slab, her death-shroud as white as a bridal gown. With a cry, Romeo rushed to her side and covered her face with kisses and tears. "I cannot live without you," he whispered. "I want your beauty to be the last thing my eyes see. We could not be together in life, my sweet love, but in death, nothing shall part us!"

Romeo drew the cork from the poison bottle and raised it to his lips. He felt the vile liquid sting his throat. Then darkness swallowed him.

For a time, there was no sound except the spluttering of the torch; then Juliet began to breathe. She moaned, opened her eyes, and saw Romeo dead at her side with the empty poison bottle in his hand. At first, she thought she was dreaming, but when she reached out to touch Romeo's face, and smelled the bitter scent of the poison, she knew that the nightmare was real, and that Friar Lawrence's plan had gone terribly wrong. She cradled Romeo in her arms and rocked

him, weeping into his hair. "If you had only waited a little longer!" she whispered, and she kissed Romeo again and again, desperately hoping that there was enough poison on his lips that she too might die.

Then she saw the torchlight gleam on the dagger at Romeo's belt. She drew the weapon and pressed its point to her heart. "Now, dagger, take me to my love!" she said, and pushed with all her strength.

Friar Lawrence found the lovers a few hours later. They were huddled together like sleeping children.

✦   ✦   ✦

When Romeo and Juliet died, the hatred between the Montagues and Capulets died with them. United by grief, the two families agreed that Romeo and Juliet should be buried together. They paid for a statue of the lovers to be set over the grave, and on the base of the statue these words were carved:

> *There never was a story of more woe*
> *Than this of Juliet and Romeo.*

The sun for sorrow will not show his head.
Go hence, to have more talk of these sad things.
THE PRINCE OF VERONA; ACT FIVE, SCENE THREE

MACBETH

The witches' prophecy brings disaster

CAST LIST

THE THREE WITCHES or Weird Sisters

MACBETH Thane of Glamis, General to King Duncan

BANQUO General to King Duncan

LADY MACBETH wife to Macbeth

A servant of Glamis Castle

KING DUNCAN King of Scotland

MALCOLM AND DONALBAIN the King's sons

Two murderers

MACDUFF Thane of Fife

THE SCENE
Scotland in the eleventh century

When shall we three meet again?
In thunder, lightning, or in rain?
When the hurly-burly's done,
When the battle's lost and won.

FIRST AND SECOND WITCHES; ACT ONE, SCENE ONE

All day, the three witches waited on the edge of the battlefield. Hidden by mist and magic, they watched the Scottish army win a victory over the invading forces of Norway, and after the fight was done they lingered on, gloating over the moans of the dying. As thunder rolled overhead and rain lashed down, one of the witches raised her long, hooked nose to the wind and sniffed like a dog taking a scent. "He will be here soon," she said.

The second witch stroked the tuft of silvery hair that sprouted from her chin, and grinned, showing her gums. "I hear the sound of hooves, sisters," she said.

The third witch held up a piece of rock crystal in front of her milky, blind eyes. Inside the crystal, something seemed to move. "I see him!" she screeched. "He comes! Let the spell begin."

Two Scottish generals rode slowly away from the battlefield, their heads lowered against the driving rain. One was Macbeth, the Thane of Glamis, the bravest soldier in King Duncan's army. He was tall, broad-shouldered and had a warrior's face, broken-nosed and scarred from old fights. His companion and friend, Banquo was younger and slimmer, with a mouth that was quick to smile, although he wasn't smiling now.

Macbeth's dark eyes were distant as he recalled the details of the day's slaughter. 'A hard fight to protect an old, feeble King', he thought. 'If I ruled Scotland…' His mind drifted off into a familiar daydream: he saw himself seated on the throne, with the golden crown of Scotland circling his brow…

Suddenly his horse reared and whinnied, its eyes rolling in terror.

Macbeth struggled to control the horse, and at that moment a bolt of lightning turned the air violet. In the eerie light he saw three weird hags barring the way, their wild hair and ragged robes streaming like tattered flags in the wind.

Macbeth's hand flew to his sword, but Banquo hissed out an urgent warning. "No, my friend! I do not think swords can harm creatures like these."

A small, cold fear entered Macbeth's heart, and he snarled to conceal it. "What do you want?" he demanded of the witches. "Stand aside!"

Moving as one, the witches raised their left arms and pointed crooked fingers at Macbeth. They spoke, and their voices grated like iron on stone.

"All hail, Macbeth, Thane of Glamis!"

"All hail, Macbeth, Thane of Cawdor!"

"All hail, Macbeth, who shall be King!"

Macbeth gave a startled gasp – how had these withered crones come to read his secret thoughts?

The witches turned their fingers to Banquo. "All hail, Banquo!" they chanted. "Your children shall be kings!"

And they vanished like a mist of breath on a mirror.

"Were they ghosts?" Banquo whispered in amazement.

"They were madwomen!" snorted Macbeth. "How can I be Thane

of Cawdor? He is alive and well and one of King Duncan's most trusted friends."

"And how could my children be kings if you took the throne?" Banquo asked.

The sound of hoofbeats made both men turn their heads. Out of the rain appeared a royal herald. He pulled his horse to a halt and lifted a hand in salute. "I bring great news!" he announced. "The Thane of Cawdor has confessed to treason and has been executed. The King has given his title and lands to you, noble Macbeth. He has proclaimed you as his heir, after his sons Malcolm and Donalbain. All hail, Macbeth, Thane of Glamis *and* Cawdor!"

Macbeth's face turned deathly pale. 'So the witches told the truth?' he thought. 'Only Duncan and his sons stand between me and the crown! My wife must know of this – I will write to her tonight.'

Macbeth was so deep in thought that he didn't notice the troubled look that Banquo gave him. The witches had left a scent of evil in the air, and Banquo seemed to smell it clinging to his friend.

+   +   +

Lady Macbeth stood at the window of her bedchamber, gazing out at the clouds gathering above the turrets of Glamis Castle. In her right hand, she held the letter from her husband, and its words echoed through her mind. "Glamis, Cawdor, King, you could have them all!" she whispered. "But I know you too well, my lord. You want greatness, but you shrink from what you must do to get it. If only…"

There was a knock at the door. Lady Macbeth started and turned, her long brown hair whispering against the green silk of her gown. "Come!" she called.

A servant entered. "A message from Lord Macbeth, my lady," he said. "He bids you prepare a royal banquet, for the King will stay at Glamis tomorrow night."

"What?" Lady Macbeth gasped in amazement. "Are you mad?"

She quickly recovered herself. "Go and tell the other servants to make ready for the King!" she commanded.

When she was alone again, Lady Macbeth opened the window, and a blast of cold air caught her hair and swirled it about her face. "Fate leads Duncan to Glamis!" she murmured. "Come to me, Powers of Darkness! Fill me with cruelty, so I may teach my husband how to be ruthless!"

A low growl of thunder answered her.

+   +   +

Macbeth rode ahead of the King's party, and arrived at Glamis just after sunrise. When his wife greeted him he noticed a hard, determined look in her eyes. "The King sleeps here tonight," he said. "Is his room ready?"

"All is ready...for Duncan's last night on Earth!" said Lady Macbeth.

"What do you mean?" Macbeth asked.

Lady Macbeth moved closer, and spoke in a low voice. "I guessed the thoughts that lay behind your letter," she said. "Duncan is old and weak. His sons are not fit to rule, but you are! Kill the King while he sleeps, and let Malcolm and Donalbain bear the blame!"

Macbeth was astonished – first the witches, and now his wife had seen his innermost thoughts. Some strange force seemed to have taken control of his life, and he fought against it. "I will never commit murder and treason!" he declared.

"I will put a sleeping-potion in a jug of wine and send it to the guards at the King's door," Lady Macbeth said quickly. "They will sleep like babes. It will be easy for you to slip into Duncan's room."

"No! I cannot!" Macbeth groaned.

Lady Macbeth's face twisted into a sneer. "This is your real chance to be King," she said. "Are you too cowardly to take it?"

"I am no coward!" snapped Macbeth.

"Then prove it!" Lady Macbeth hissed. "Kill the old man and take the throne!"

Once more, the strange force moved through Macbeth,

flowing into him from his wife until he was unable to resist. 'All hail, Macbeth, who shall be King!' he thought, and he could almost feel the crown upon his head.

+   +   +

Long after the castle had fallen silent, Macbeth left his room and crept along the corridors. His hands trembled, and the sound of his pulse in his ears was like the beating of a battle drum. 'This is the hour of the wolf and the witch,' he thought, 'when evil spirits roam the night.'

And as the words crossed his mind, a ghostly glow gathered in

the darkness, shaping itself into a dagger that floated in the air, shining with a sickly green light. Macbeth almost cried out in terror. "Be calm!" he told himself. "This is a trick of the mind!" To prove it, he reached out his hand to take the dagger, but it floated away from him and pointed the way to Duncan's door. Blood began to ooze from the blade, as though the iron were weeping red tears.

A bell tolled midnight.

"Duncan's funeral bell is ringing!" muttered Macbeth, and he followed the dagger through the gloom.

+   +   +

Lady Macbeth also heard the bell toll, and it seemed a long time before her husband returned. There was blood on his face and hands, and he carried two daggers.

"You should not have brought the daggers here!" said Lady Macbeth.

"Go back and put them into the guards' hands, as we planned!"

Macbeth's eyes were blank. He shook his head. "I will not go back there!" he said hoarsely.

"Then *I will!*" said Lady Macbeth, and snatched the daggers from Macbeth's hands and left the room.

Macbeth stood where he was, shivering uncontrollably, seeing nothing but Duncan's dead eyes staring. He tried to pray, but his lips and tongue would not form the words.

In a short while, Lady Macbeth came back, holding her red hands up to the candle-light. "I smeared blood over the guards' faces, to make them seem guilty," she said. "In the morning, we will have them tortured until they say that Duncan's sons paid them to kill him!"

Her face was so full of triumph and cruelty, that Macbeth no longer recognised it. He turned away, and caught sight of his reflection in the mirror. It was as if he were looking at someone else – as if he and his wife had become strangers to themselves and each other.

✦   ✦   ✦

Glamis Castle was woken in the grey light of dawn by voices shouting, "Murder! The King is slain!" Shocked guests ran from their rooms and spoke in whispers. Who could have murdered the King? Rumours flew through the castle like swallows – and suspicion fell on Malcolm and Donalbain, who had the most to gain from their father's death.

Malcolm and Donalbain

were convinced that Macbeth was the murderer, but they did not dare
to accuse him – who would believe that the hero of the battle against
the Norwegians would slay his own King? Though they knew it would
be taken as proof of their guilt, Duncan's sons fled for their lives.
Donalbain sailed for Ireland, and Malcolm rode across the border into
England, to put himself under the protection of the English King.

Now nothing stood between Macbeth and the throne. He was
crowned, but the crown did not bring him the pleasure he had imagined.
His secret dream had come true, but he was disturbed by other dreams –
dreams of what the witches had foretold for Banquo's descendants.
'Have I lied and murdered to set Banquo's spawn on the throne?'
he brooded. 'I must find a way to rid myself of him, and his son.'

A dark plan formed in Macbeth's mind, and he kept it a secret – even
from Lady Macbeth. Without either of them realising, the strange force
that had compelled them to kill Duncan was slowly driving them apart.

+   +   +

Macbeth held a coronation feast in the royal castle at Dunsinane. Many
of the nobles who attended remarked that Macbeth's old friend, Banquo,
was not present, but Macbeth laughed when they mentioned it. "Lord
Banquo and his son must have been delayed on their way," he said lightly.
Only he knew what had delayed them, for he had hired two murderers
to ambush them on the road.

At the height of the feast, a servant brought Macbeth a message that
two men wished to see him on urgent business. Macbeth hurried to
his private chambers, and found the murderers waiting there.

"Have you done what I paid you to do?" Macbeth demanded.

"Banquo is dead, my lord," one of the murderers said. "We cut
his throat and threw the body into a ditch."

Macbeth sighed with relief – perhaps now he would sleep peacefully.
But then he sensed something wrong: neither of the murderers
would look at him, and they kept anxiously shuffling their feet.

"And his son?" said Macbeth.

The reply was shattering. "He escaped, my lord. Banquo's son still lives."

As he returned to the banqueting hall, doubts tortured Macbeth like scorpions' stings. 'Banquo's son still lives!' he thought. 'Lives to take his revenge on me, to claim the throne and father sons who will rule after him. Is there no end to the blood that must be shed before I find peace?'

As he entered the hall, Macbeth put on a false smile to hide his troubled mind; but the smile froze when he saw a hooded figure seated in his chair. "Who dares to sit in my place?" he roared.

The guests fell silent and looked bewildered: the King's chair was empty.

"Why…no one, my lord!" said Lady Macbeth, with a forced laugh. She could see that something was wrong with her husband, but she could not guess what. "The King is jesting!" she told the nobles.

"This is no jest!" barked Macbeth. He strode angrily towards the figure, then recoiled in horror as it drew back its hood.

For what he saw was Banquo – with weed tangled in his hair, and mud streaked across his face, with a deep gash in his neck that sent a stream of blood pattering onto the flagstones and haunting, glassy eyes that stared and stared.

"Get rid of him!" Macbeth screeched.

The nobles sprang to their feet, drawing their daggers, knocking over chairs and wine cups in the confusion.

"Back to your grave!" sobbed Macbeth.

Banquo smiled – there was blood in his mouth, and his teeth shone white through it, then he faded into the shadows and the torchlight.

"My lords, the King is ill," Lady Macbeth said desperately. "Leave us now, and let him rest. In the morning, he will be himself again."

"Myself?" Macbeth moaned softly to himself. "I will not be myself again until Banquo's spirit is laid to rest. Only the witches can set me free!"

✦　　　✦　　　✦

The witches were seated in a huddle around a fire, over which a cauldron bubbled. In the sky above their heads a full moon sailed, casting silver light over the battlefield, still littered with unburied corpses.

The blind witch held up her crystal. Deep inside, a tiny horse and rider galloped wildly through the night. "He comes!" she cackled. "The spell is still strong!"

And Macbeth came out of the moonlight, his horse's flanks white with lathered sweat. He climbed from the saddle and was about to speak when the hook-nosed witch called out, "The King wishes to know the future!"

"It is not for the faint-hearted!" warned the bearded witch.

"I have courage enough!" Macbeth growled.

The blind witch dipped a wooden cup into the cauldron, and held it out. "Drink!" she said.

Macbeth took the cup and lifted it to his lips, shuddering as he swallowed. Fire, and ice, and the light of the moon burned in his brain.

The blind witch's face melted like the edge of a cloud, and became the face of Duncan, his silver hair dark with blood. "Beware Macduff, the Thane of Fife!" Duncan said, and then he changed into Banquo. "No man born of a woman can harm you," Banquo said. "You will rule until Birnam Wood walks to Dunsinane."

"Then I am safe!" cried Macbeth. "No one can stop me!"

And he was alone: the witches, their cauldron and the fire had vanished.

It was the start of a fearful time. On his return to Dunsinane, Macbeth ordered that Macduff be arrested. When he heard that Macduff had fled to England to join Malcolm, Macbeth had Macduff's castle burned, and his wife and children put to death. From then on, anyone who questioned the King's commands – no matter how harsh or unjust those commands might be – was executed.

The gap between Macbeth and his wife grew wider. The guilty secret of Duncan's murder gnawed at Lady Macbeth's mind like a maggot inside an apple. She fell ill and began to walk in her sleep, dreaming that she and Macbeth were still covered with Duncan's blood. "Out, damned stain!" she croaked. "Will nothing make me clean?" Doctors could do nothing for her, and she grew weaker every day.

Then at last hope came to Macbeth's suffering subjects. Malcolm had raised an army in England and, with Macduff at his side, he marched his troops into Scotland. There the army was greeted by cheering crowds, who longed to be freed from the tyrant Macbeth.

First Glamis Castle was captured and burned, and then Malcolm's forces marched on to Dunsinane. To the despair of Macbeth's generals, he did nothing. Each time they advised him to go to battle, he laughed and said, "I have nothing to fear until the day that Birnam Wood walks to Dunsinane."

Through the windows of the throne room, Macbeth could see the distant campfires of Malcolm's army. He raised a cup of wine to them. "Fools!" he jeered. "You cannot overthrow me!"

A sound made him turn. A servant was standing at the door, wringing his hands and weeping.

"What is it?" Macbeth asked gruffly.

"The Queen, my lord," said the servant. "She is…dead."

For a long time, Macbeth was silent, remembering the early years of his marriage, when the world had seemed bright. "Life goes on, day after day, but it means nothing," he said in a cracked whisper. "It ends in despair, and darkness…and death."

Macbeth did not sleep that night. He drank cup after cup of wine, but it brought him no comfort. Only the certainty that his enemies would be defeated and that he would remain unharmed, gave him any hope.

At dawn, an anxious-faced captain brought the King strange news. "The enemy is approaching, my lord," he said. "To conceal the strength of their numbers, they are hiding behind branches cut from Birnam Wood. It looks as though a forest is on the march."

"My curse upon you, witches!" howled Macbeth. "You deceived me! I have lost everything, but at least I can die like a soldier, with a sword in my hand! Go tell the servants to bring my armour!"

✝   ✝   ✝

It was a short battle. Macbeth's army had no stomach for a fight to protect a king they now hated, and the soldiers began to surrender to Malcolm's men – first in a trickle, then in a flood.

Macbeth fought recklessly, as though he wished to be killed, but he hacked down opponent after opponent, shouting, "You were born of woman!" as he delivered the death blow.

At last, Macbeth found himself alone. He was resting against a cart, when he heard someone call his name. It was Macduff, striding through the smoke of battle, his broadsword at the ready. "I have come to avenge my wife and children!" Macduff said through clenched teeth.

"Stay back!" warned Macbeth. "I cannot be harmed by a man born of woman."

"My mother died before I was born," said Macduff, his eyes blazing with hate. "To save me, the doctor cut me from her body."

Macbeth threw back his head and laughed bitterly. He saw now that all the witches' promises had been lies, and that by believing them, he had betrayed himself. The force that had dominated him was gone, and only his courage remained. "Come then, Macduff!" he cried. "Make an end of me!"

Macduff struck off Macbeth's head with a single sweep of his sword.

+   +   +

The head was placed on top of a spear that had been driven into the ground outside the gates of Dunsinane. The victorious army cheered, then marched away to see Malcolm crowned King.

As the sun set, three ravens flapped down from the castle walls and fluttered around Macbeth's head. "All hail, Macbeth!" they cawed. "All hail! All hail!"

Out, out, brief candle.
Life's but a walking shadow, a poor player
That struts and frets his hour upon the stage,
And then is heard no more.
MACBETH; ACT FIVE, SCENE FIVE

ANTONY AND CLEOPATRA

The love that destroyed an Empire

CAST LIST

SERVIUS storyteller, a bodyguard to Antony

MARK ANTONY one of the three rulers of Rome

CLEOPATRA Queen of Egypt

OCTAVIUS CAESAR AND LEPIDUS rulers of Rome with Antony

Antony's Generals

THE SCENE
Ancient Egypt and Rome

Eternity was in our lips and eyes,
Bliss in our brow's bent; none our parts so poor
But was a race of heaven.
CLEOPATRA; ACT ONE, SCENE THREE

You want to know about Antony and Cleopatra? Let me tell you the story – the *real* story.

I was there at the start, the night Julius Caesar was killed and Antony made a speech over his body in the Market Place. As soon as he stood before us, pale and proud in the torchlight, my heart went out to him. He spoke in a voice like the beating of a war drum, and by the time he had finished speaking, I knew I would follow him anywhere – to the shores of Hades and beyond, if he asked me to. When civil war broke out, I was one of the first to join Antony's legions.

It was a bitter, bloody struggle: Roman against Roman, each believing that right was on his side. I was commended for my courage in action – though all I did was keep my head and obey orders – and Antony himself promoted me to the rank of centurion, just before the battle of Philippi. That's where I got this scar on my neck, but I was lucky. Braver men than I died that day, including Brutus, who killed himself to escape the shame of defeat. Antony wept at the sight of Brutus's corpse, and many of us wept with him.

Then came the peace, though few believed that it would last. The Empire was carved like a goose, and divided up between the three victors. War makes for strange alliances, but none as strange as that trio. Octavius Caesar, Julius Caesar's nephew, was as ruthless and cold as Antony was warm and generous; Lepidus, the third ally, was a joke – a jellyfish with no sting. Caesar took the West, Antony the East, and Lepidus the African provinces that were left over.

Almost straightaway there was trouble in the East. The Parthians invaded Roman territory, and Antony sailed out with his legions to deal with them. There was a battle – of sorts. The Parthians were poorly armed, and undisciplined; most of them turned and ran the moment they saw the sunlight shining on our shields.

After the victory, Antony called me to his tent. "Well, Servius," he said, "your centurion days are over."

I thought he was going to pension me off and send me back to Rome. "Why, sir?" I protested.

Antony gave me one of his boyish grins. "Because I want you to join my bodyguard," he said. "I need good fighters about me, men I can trust – and I know I can rely on you."

I was lost for words. My heart beat so proudly that I thought it would burst my armour.

"We leave for Tarsus tonight," Antony said. "I have commanded Queen Cleopatra of Egypt to meet me there, to answer charges that she supplied Brutus with troops and money. I want you at my side. I wouldn't put it past her to slip a hired assassin into the crowds."

"While I've breath in my body, no assassin will get past me to strike at you, sir," I said, and I meant every word.

There was gossip on the road to Tarsus, all of it about Cleopatra, and little of it worth repeating. Men said she was a beauty, who had charmed Julius Caesar and made him fawn over her like a dog. Now, the story went, she planned to do the same with Antony, but I would have none of it. "Caesar was past his prime," I said. "Antony is still young, and his wife is a member of one of Rome's most powerful families. It will take more than some Egyptian woman to make him forget where his loyalty lies, even if she is a queen."

How the Gods must have laughed when they heard that!

A few days later, I was on the quayside at Tarsus with Antony, waiting for Cleopatra's royal barge to arrive. It was more than two hours late, and Antony was annoyed. "This is an insult!" he kept muttering.

"That little Nile serpent means to make me look a fool!"

But at last we heard distant voices on the wind: women's

voices, singing a twisting, slithering melody that my ears could not follow. Cleopatra's barge rounded a bend in the river, and the watching crowds gasped.

The hull, deck and oars of the barge had been gilded, so that the boat looked like a fire burning on the water. The sails were deep purple and scented and the breeze that filled them carried the fragrance across the harbour. I breathed in the perfume of Egypt for the first time: a spicy, honeyed smell that made my head swim.

The barge drew close, and I caught my first glimpse of Cleopatra. Her robes were cloth of gold, and she wore the double crown of Egypt. Her skin was golden-brown, her hair black, and glossy as a horse's flank; her huge, dark eyes were deep and still. I had heard tales that Helen of Troy was the most beautiful woman ever, but when I saw Cleopatra, I knew that Helen had been eclipsed.

"This is no Queen!" Antony said softly. "This is a Goddess!"

Cleopatra stepped onto the quay, and the cheering crowds sounded like storm waves breaking.

Antony stepped forward and said, "In the name of the Senate and People of Rome, I greet you, and require you to…" He broke off in astonishment as Cleopatra knelt at his feet and bowed her head.

The crowds fell silent.

Antony frowned, then bent down, and helped Cleopatra to her feet. "My noble lord does me too much honour," she said, her head still lowered.

"There is much to discuss," said Antony, "but this is not a fit place. Dine with me tonight, in the city."

"No, my lord," Cleopatra said.

'No' was not a word that Antony was used to hearing, and I saw him stiffen in anger; but then Cleopatra looked up at him. "Dine with me, on the barge," she said. "Let me see if my Egyptian cooks can please you. Eat with me and taste new delights, my lord."

Antony looked into Cleopatra's eyes, and his anger melted. "Now I am the honoured one," he said.

I knew then that he had fallen in love with her, as surely as if I had seen one of Eros's arrows pierce his heart.

Within a week, we set sail for Egypt, and nothing was ever the same again.

+   +   +

Egypt was another world. Beyond the Nile's green valley stretched the desert, unchanging and timeless. In Egypt, the years slipped away like a handful of water.

Antony grew older and softer. He seemed to care for nothing but

Cleopatra and their children. Some of the soldiers became restless, saying that Antony was not the man he had once been, and that Cleopatra had bewitched him. Such talk made me angry. "You'll see Antony's greatness again when the time comes!" I said.

And the time came. There was chaos in Rome: Antony's wife, Fulvia, and Lucius, his brother, raised an army to overthrow Octavius Caesar and were crushed in battle. Fulvia died on her way to see Antony in Egypt. At the same time, Sextus Pompeius rebelled against Caesar, and the Parthians invaded the Roman territories at their borders.

The world of Rome seemed about to collapse.

I was with Antony when the dispatches reached him. His face darkened as he read them, and for a long time he brooded in silence. "Is it true, Servius?" he asked at last. "Am I really as old and weak as they say?"

"You are Mark Antony, sir," I told him.

Something of his old look shone in Antony's eyes. "I will go to Rome and settle my differences with Caesar," he said. "If he, I and Lepidus make peace with Pompeius, we can put our forces together, defeat the Parthians and save Rome before it is too late." Then his face fell. "But what shall I tell the Queen?" he murmured.

Cleopatra stormed, and wept and pleaded, but at last she saw that she had no choice but to let Antony go. She feared he would not return, but I knew that his love for her was too strong for him to keep away for very long.

✦   ✦   ✦

In Rome, Antony was a grizzled lion, Caesar a cold and haughty eagle, and Lepidus a crab, scurrying beside them. They talked behind locked doors, late into the night and standing guard outside, I heard Antony and Caesar raise their voices in anger, while Lepidus twittered and whined.

Antony emerged from the chamber looking tired and worried. He took me aside and said, "I want you to leave for Egypt at once. Tell the Queen that I have made my peace with Caesar."

I frowned: this was good news – yet Antony's face was troubled.

"But the peace came at a price," he went on. "To strengthen the alliance, I must marry Octavia, Caesar's sister. Tell the Queen that the marriage means nothing, and that my love for her is unchanged. I will return to Egypt with Octavia when we have signed a treaty with Pompeius."

Doubts rose in my mind like a flock of crows. All Rome knew how dearly Caesar loved his sister. How long would it be before he discovered that her marriage to Antony was a sham? It would be all the excuse he needed to declare war and try to seize the whole Empire for himself. And when Cleopatra heard of the marriage, who could tell what she might do? I glimpsed Antony's future, and it was all blood and shadows.

✦   ✦   ✦

I had no flowery words to decorate Antony's message. I spoke out like a soldier, blunt and plain.

Cleopatra's rage was furious. "Tell me that you are lying, or you shall be whipped with wire and boiled in salted water!" she shrieked.

"Madam, I speak the truth," I said. "Antony is married to Octavia."

Cleopatra drew a knife; I do not know whether she intended to stab me or herself, for one of her handmaidens snatched the knife away. Cleopatra shook her head, scattering tears that gleamed as they fell. "Then let Egypt sink into the Nile!" she moaned. "Let the sky fall and crush the Earth!"

Egypt did not sink, nor did the sky fall, but one terrible happening led to another.

Before Antony and Octavia were halfway to Egypt, Caesar broke the treaty with Pompeius, defeated him in battle, seized the African provinces and had Lepidus put to death. Antony knew that war was coming, and sent Octavia back to Rome, being too honourable a man to keep her as a hostage.

Once Antony was back in Egypt, he and Cleopatra joined forces against Caesar. Though their love remained strong, some of the fire between them had dwindled because of Antony's marriage of convenience.

Antony seemed his old self again, confident and decisive; but also headstrong, as if age had made him stubborn instead of wise. Against all advice, he insisted on a battle at sea, to prevent Caesar from landing his troops.

Antony's generals were in despair. "This is madness, sir!" one of them was brave enough to tell him. "The enemy ships greatly outnumber ours. If we lose the fleet, we cannot keep our troops supplied. Fight Caesar on land!"

"Let no man say that Antony feared to face an enemy," Antony replied. "I will meet Caesar at sea!"

Actium, they called that battle. I still dream of it, and wake up shouting. The ships fired flaming pitch and sulphur at one another. Burning men leapt screaming into the sea and when two ships came alongside, soldiers from each tried to board the other, so the decks ran red.

For a time, it seemed that Antony might be victorious; then love betrayed him. Cleopatra sailed out in her barge, thinking that the sight of her would encourage Antony and the Egyptian fleet; but the horror and slaughter of the battle made her order the barge back to harbour. A Roman galley broke formation to give chase, and Antony turned his ship around to go to Cleopatra's rescue. When the captains of the fleet saw their commander leave the fight, they believed that all was lost, and fled.

After the disaster at Actium, Antony bargained for peace. He offered Caesar his third of the Empire, in return for being allowed to stay in Egypt with the Queen. Caesar refused: he would make peace with Cleopatra, he said, but only if Antony were executed.

Antony accused Cleopatra of betraying him, out of spite for his marriage to Octavia. Cleopatra was terrified by Antony's fury, and went into hiding.

The generals had their land battle in the end – outside the walls of Alexandria. We fought like heroes, and Caesar's men fell like wheat to the scythe. But even as the celebrations began in Antony's tent, a messenger arrived with grave news. The Egyptian fleet had surrendered; Antony could no longer keep his army fed and armed; the war was lost.

Antony ordered everyone from the tent, except me. When we were alone, he drew his sword and offered it to me, hilt first.

"Kill me, Servius," he said. "I cannot bear to beg Caesar for mercy."

"Sir," I said, "I know where the Queen is hiding. You could be with her in an hour. You could escape to…"

"To live in fear until Caesar hunts us down?" said Antony. "No, Servius. I am finished. Take the sword and end it."

"Not I, sir!" I said. "I would gladly die for you, but I will not do what you ask."

"Then by my own hand be it," said Antony.

 He stabbed with both hands, but the point of the sword slipped on his breastbone and ran into his belly. He pulled out

the sword and threw it across the tent with a cry of disgust, knowing that his death would be long and painful. Agony drove him to his knees. "Cleopatra!" he gasped. "Take me to her!"

I do not know how Antony found the strength to stand, and mount a horse, but as night fell we rode across the desert to Cleopatra's hiding place: her own tomb, built in the shape of a crouching lion with a man's head. I beat against the doors, my shouts echoing off the stone, until a slave answered, and drew back the bolts. Antony leaned on me, and we staggered inside.

The tomb was lit by a hundred oil lamps that shone on the richly decorated walls. Paintings of Egyptian Gods stared down with sightless, animal eyes. Cleopatra was seated on a throne, dressed in her royal robes. A reed basket stood at her feet, and I remember thinking it a poor thing to find in such a place.

Cleopatra saw the blood from Antony's wound, and ran to him. We gently laid him down. Cleopatra sat, and rested his head on her lap.

"I am dying, Egypt," Antony said. "Tell Caesar you had me killed, and make peace with him."

"Never!" said Cleopatra.

Antony's face clenched in pain. "Then add one more kiss to the thousands you have given me," he said.

Cleopatra lowered her head, pressed her lips to Antony's, and he was gone.

"The sun has burned out," Cleopatra whispered. "The world is dark."

Tears clouded my eyes. I did not see the Queen stand, or reach into the basket and take out the small black snake coiled within it. When I could see again, she was on her throne, and the snake's fangs were sunk deep in her breast. "Sweet as perfume!" she said. "Soft as air! Oh, Antony!"

And so her life ended.

✦   ✦   ✦

And that's my story. It will be told and retold, until time ends. Antony and Cleopatra will always be together, though their beauty and greatness turned to desert dust long ago.

They say that in the East, Emperor Octavius Caesar is worshipped as a God. Well, if Caesar is a God, then let my death come soon, for the world is past my understanding.

But Antony – now there was a man!

She shall be buried by her Antony.
No grave upon the earth shall clip in it
A pair so famous.
CAESAR; ACT FIVE, SCENE TWO

TWELFTH NIGHT

A mixed-up romance

CAST LIST

SEBASTIAN AND VIOLA twin brother and sister

ORSINO Duke of Illyria

SIR TOBY BELCH uncle to Olivia

SIR ANDREW AGUECHEEK friend to Sir Toby

OLIVIA a rich Countess

MALVOLIO steward to Olivia

A sailor

THE SCENE
Coastal Illyria, fifteenth century

If music be the food of love, play on,
Give me excess of it.
ORSINO; ACT ONE, SCENE ONE

Sebastian and his twin sister Viola were as alike as two raindrops. They had the same light brown hair, bright blue eyes and winning smiles. Sometimes, when they were children, Viola used to borrow Sebastian's clothes and pretend to be him – which confused everybody.

The twins grew up together, were taught together, and they almost died together. That was on the day the ship in which they were travelling foundered on a treacherous reef and sank. Viola saved herself by clinging to Sebastian's clothes-trunk, and was washed up on the coast of Illyria. As she was a practical, quick-thinking person, Viola decided she would be safer if she disguised herself as a young man, so she tied up her hair, dressed in clothes that she took from her brother's trunk and called herself Cesario. She prayed that Sebastian had survived the shipwreck and for three days she sought news of him, but then her money ran out, so, still disguised as Cesario, she found a job as a page to Duke Orsino, ruler of Illyria.

✦   ✦   ✦

Orsino was delighted with his new page, and before long, Viola had won his confidence, and he had won her heart. The Duke was tall, dark, handsome, rich, and popular with his people – and yet he was not content. He moped about his palace during the day, and in the evening listened to troubadours singing sad songs. He never laughed, and hardly ever smiled.

Like many young women before her, Viola found herself falling in love with Orsino and it was painful to keep her feelings a secret. The pain became even worse when, one day when they were alone together, she summoned up the courage to ask why he was so unhappy.

"Because I am suffering from the worst sickness in the world – love!"

Orsino replied. "I'm so in love with Countess Olivia that I don't know what to do, Cesario! I've asked her to marry me a dozen times, but she keeps refusing."

"She must be mad!" said Viola. "If you asked me to – I mean, if I were a woman, I would marry you at once, my lord!"

Orsino sighed, then suddenly he had an idea that seemed so brilliant, that for a moment he looked almost happy. "You know, Cesario, I think you could gain Olivia's trust as quickly as you have gained mine," he said thoughtfully. "Go and see her today. Tell her that if she won't marry me, I'll waste away and die!"

"Me, my lord?" gulped Viola.

Orsino placed his hand on Viola's shoulder. "You're my last hope!"

'So I must try and persuade Countess Olivia to marry the man I love!' Viola thought ruefully. 'Why does life have to be so complicated?'

Though she did not realise it at that moment, Viola's life was about to become more complicated than she could possibly imagine.

✦ ✦ ✦

Countess Olivia's parents had died when she was still young and her uncle, Sir Toby Belch had come to live with her. Sir Toby was short and plump, with white whiskers and twinkling blue eyes, and his love of wine and good food had turned his nose bright red. His closest friend was Sir Andrew Aguecheek, a man with a face as long and wrinkled as a bloodhound's, and, since Sir Andrew was a bachelor, Sir Toby had decided that he would make the perfect husband for his niece, Olivia. However, Olivia's steward, Malvolio protected her from all unwanted suitors, including Sir Andrew!

On the day that Orsino sent Viola to plead with Olivia, Sir Toby and Sir Andrew were plotting together in the library of Olivia's house.

"If I could only be alone with her for five minutes!" Sir Andrew grumbled. "But Malvolio will not let me see her. He won't even give her my letters."

"My niece has given him far too much control of her affairs, and it's gone to his head," grumbled Sir Tony. "Why, the other evening, the scoundrel actually had the impudence to tell me that I drink too much!"

"The villain!" said Sir Andrew.

"But I intend to teach him a lesson," Sir Toby said, with a mischievous grin. "Mark my words, old friend, before the day is over, Malvolio will be out of your way."

✦   ✦   ✦

While her uncle schemed in the library, Olivia was strolling in the garden with Malvolio at her side. With his skinny body and black clothes, Malvolio resembled a bony shadow. "A young man called Cesario wishes to see you, my lady," he was saying to her. "He brings a message from the Duke Orsino."

"Tell him to go away!" said Olivia, and her green eyes flashed as she tossed her dark-red hair in irritation.

"I have, my lady," said Malvolio. "But he says he will stand at the gate all afternoon if he has to." Malvolio sniffed haughtily. "He is a most insolent young fellow!"

"Oh, let me see him, then!" Olivia said wearily. "Perhaps, when he hears my reply, Orsino will finally abandon all hope of marrying me!"

When Viola entered the garden, Olivia pretended to be interested in the blossoms on a rose bush, and gave Orsino's new messenger no more than a glance.

"Sweet lady," said Viola. "Now I see how beautiful you are, I understand why my master is so in love with you!"

Olivia, who hated flattery of any kind, snorted scornfully. "Beautiful?" she said. "I have two eyes, a nose and a mouth like everybody else, if that's what you mean!"

"Ah, so you are proud as well as lovely!" said Viola. "It is a pity that the Duke loves a lady with such a hard heart."

"Orsino doesn't really love me!" Olivia declared. "He's just in love with the idea of being in love. Go and tell him I cannot make myself love

him just because he wants me to!" She looked up from the roses, and as she did so, she saw quite the most beautiful young man she had ever met. Her head swam giddily and her heart began to pound. "Tell Orsino that I will never marry him," she said breathlessly. "And then…come back to see me at once, Cesario."

"Why?" frowned Viola.

"Er…to tell me how he responds to my answer!" Olivia said with a blush.

Viola bowed and turned to go, leaving Olivia alone with a whirlwind of thoughts and feelings she had never experienced before. One moment, Olivia wanted to laugh out loud, and the next, she wanted to burst into tears. She was so confused, that she did not notice Malvolio approaching. He seemed to drop out of the sky and land in front of her.

"I hope that young man did not offend you, my lady?" Malvolio said.

"Offend me?" said Olivia. "Why, no. I mean – yes, yes he did!" On impulse, she pulled a ring from one of her fingers. "He brought me this gift from the Duke. Return the ring to Cesario and tell him I don't want it!"

"Of course, my lady," Malvolio said smoothly. "Where is the fellow?"

"Gone," said Olivia. "If you run, you'll soon catch up with him."

"What, run – I?" gasped Malvolio; then he bowed politely as he saw the angry green fire in Olivia's eyes. "I'll go at once!" he said.

+   +   +

Viola walked slowly. Her heart was heavy for Orsino, and herself, and when a voice from behind called out, "Cesario?" for a moment she forgot that it was the name she had given herself, and did not remember until the voice called out again. "Cesario! Ho, there!"

Viola turned and saw Malvolio running towards her, his elbows sticking out and his knobbly knees pumping up and down. This was surprise enough, but Viola was completely astonished when Malvolio offered her a ring. "You brought my lady this!"

he panted. "Now she wants you to take it back."

"I didn't give her a ring!" said Viola.

Malvolio peevishly stamped his foot and threw the ring to the ground. "Let it lie there, then!" he snapped. "I have better things to do than argue with the likes of you!" He turned on his heel and marched angrily away.

Viola stooped and picking up the ring, saw on it a design of two hands holding a heart. 'But this is a love token!' she thought. 'Young women don't send love tokens to other young women!' The truth fell on her like an avalanche. "Oh, no!" she cried. "Olivia thinks I'm a man – and she's fallen in love with me!"

✦   ✦   ✦

Orsino was alone when Viola found him. He was singing a song about doomed lovers and how, no matter how brightly the sun shone, somewhere the rain was sure to be pouring down like tears. Viola waited until the song was over, then told Orsino what Olivia had said.

Orsino closed his eyes. "Ah!" he groaned tragically. "If you knew what agony love can be, Cesario!"

"Oh, I do, my lord!" Viola said.

Orsino unpinned a brooch from his doublet and handed it to Viola. "Then go to Olivia again," he said. "Give her this brooch and tell her that even though she will not be my wife, my love will last as long as the diamonds that are set into it!"

✦   ✦   ✦

Meanwhile Malvolio had returned to the garden. Olivia was not there, but as he hurried towards the house to find her, he found a letter lying on the path and picked it up. "Why, this is my lady's handwriting!" Malvolio murmured. "Since I am her steward, and her business is my business, it is my duty to read it!" He was so interested in the letter

 that he failed to see Sir Toby and Sir Andrew, hidden in a bank of laurel bushes nearby.

"*To M, my dearest love,*" Malvolio read aloud. "*Though you are my servant, you are master of my heart. Be bold, and my hand is yours! If you love me, wear yellow tights, cross-gartered, as a secret sign.*" Malvolio clutched the letter to his bosom. "Olivia loves me!" he burbled. "I must change into yellow tights at once!"

As soon as Malvolio was out of sight, the laurel bushes began to shake with laughter. "I knew it would work!" Sir Toby told Sir Andrew. "I can imitate my niece's handwriting well enough to deceive anybody! Now all we have to do is…"

"Hush!" said Sir Andrew. "Someone is coming!"

✦   ✦   ✦

Olivia and Viola were deep in conversation. They stopped in front of a bank of laurel bushes, and Viola said, "Then you have no new answer for the Duke?"

"No!" said Olivia, clutching Viola's hand. "But there are answers I would give to you, Cesario, if you would only ask me the questions!"

Viola gently took her hand away. "My lady, I am not all that I seem to be," she said tactfully.

"But I love you!" exclaimed Olivia. "I loved you from the first moment I set eyes on you."

"You might as well love a dream," Viola said. "You must forget me, my lady!" and she slipped away, leaving Olivia in tears.

In the bushes, Sir Andrew quivered with rage. "That chit of a youth has stolen Olivia's love!" he hissed.

"After him!" urged Sir Toby. "Challenge him to a duel! That should see him off!"

"A duel?" said Sir Andrew, alarmed.

"He won't dare to fight you!" said Sir Toby. "That Cesario is nothing but a puny milksop – he'll turn tail and run the moment you draw your sword!"

While Sir Andrew went to waylay Viola at the garden gate, Olivia stumbled towards the house, her eyes filled with tears. "Oh, Cesario!" she whispered. "I must see you again, if only for a second!"

Then she saw Malvolio walking towards her. He was wearing yellow tights as bright as canaries, and his face was stretched into a ghastly smile. "Well met, my angel!" he simpered.

"Malvolio?" said Olivia. "Are you feeling quite well?"

"Never better, my sweetness!" Malvolio purred, stretching out his right leg. "Have you noticed my yellow tights and cross-garters?"

"I could hardly miss them!" Olivia replied. "I think the heat has made you feverish. Wouldn't you like to lie down?"

"Yes, with you by my side!" said Malvolio.

"Help!" cried Olivia. "Servants, take Malvolio away! He has lost his wits!"

+   +   +

Meanwhile, Viola, relieved to be going back to her master, the Duke, suddenly found herself face to face with a furious Sir Andrew Aguecheek.

"Draw your sword, vile scoundrel!" snarled Sir Andrew.

"My sword?" Viola quailed. "But why?"

"So I can fight you!" Sir Andrew said. "Or are you a coward as well as a villain?"

Reluctantly, Viola reached for her sword with a trembling hand, and at that same moment, most fortunately a loud voice shouted, "Stop!"

A hefty sailor appeared through the gateway.

"If you harm one hair of this young man's head," he warned Sir Andrew, "I'll carve you up like a joint of beef!"

"Oh!" said Sir Andrew, pale with fear. "Oh, well in that case, I think I'd better…" and he ran away at an impressive speed.

Viola felt weak with relief. "How can I ever thank you, kind stranger?" she said to the sailor.

"Stranger?" scowled the sailor. "That's a fine thing to call the man who saved you from drowning and helped you to try and find your lost sister! I've been waiting for you at the inn down the road for the last two days, Sebastian!"

"*Sebastian?*" gasped Viola. "Then my brother is alive and well!"

+   +   +

Sebastian was alive and well, but totally bewildered. On his way to meet the sailor who had saved him, he happened to pass a fine house out of which rushed a beautiful red-haired young woman. "I knew you would come back, Cesario!" she said, flinging her arms around him. "We cannot live without each other!"

"But, my lady," Sebastian said.

"Call me Olivia, my dearest!" said Olivia.

Sebastian looked into Olivia's eyes. He was about to tell her that she had made a terrible mistake, and that his name was not Cesario, but then his heart began to beat faster as love worked its magic on him. "This must be a dream!" he said softly. "But please, don't wake me up yet!" And he hugged Olivia tightly.

The two of them were still embracing when Viola and the sailor discovered them. Sebastian recognised his sister and ran to her with a joyous shout. He lifted Viola high into the air, while Olivia and the sailor looked on open-mouthed.

"Are there two of him?" whispered Olivia. "I don't understand."

"It seems so," said the sailor, scratching his head. "If you ask me, my lady, someone has a lot of explaining to do!"

+   +   +

Duke Orsino waited two anxious hours for Cesario to return, and at last he lost his patience. He called for his fastest horse, and galloped to Olivia's house. In the hall, he was met with the strangest sight – Cesario and Olivia,

arm in arm, and behind them, a smiling priest holding a bible.

"Cesario!" Orsino thundered. "Release that lady!"

"This is not Cesario, my lord," Olivia beamed. "This is Sebastian, who will soon be my husband. If you seek the one you called Cesario, look behind you!"

Orsino turned and saw Viola, wearing a dress that Olivia had lent her. She looked so lovely that she quite took Orsino's breath away, and he instantly fell head over heels in love with her.

"If you take my advice, you'll marry her straightaway," Olivia told the Duke. "She loves you with all her heart!"

"And now I see her as her rightful self, I love her with all mine!" Orsino declared.

✦   ✦   ✦

And so there was a double wedding in the house of Countess Olivia, and that night the windows were bright with lights, and the air was filled with the sounds of music and celebration.

The laughter and singing rang through the house, and reached the ears of Malvolio, who had been locked in the cellar. He pressed his face against the bars of the window and called out, "Hello, hello! Let me out, someone! I am not mad – truly I am not!"

But nobody heard him, not that night.

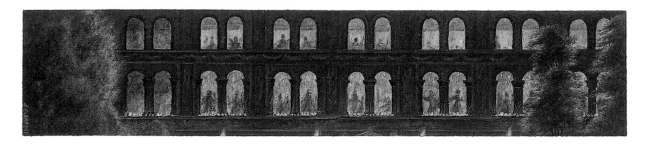

I'll follow this good man, and go with you,
And having sworn truth, ever will be true.
SEBASTIAN; ACT FIVE, SCENE ONE

HAMLET, PRINCE OF DENMARK

A traitor is avenged

CAST LIST

HAMLET son to the former King, nephew to Claudius

HORATIO friend to Hamlet

The ghost of Hamlet's father

OPHELIA daughter to Polonius

A troop of travelling players

CLAUDIUS King of Denmark

GERTRUDE Queen of Denmark and mother to Hamlet

POLONIUS Lord Chamberlain

LAERTES son to Polonius

THE SCENE
Denmark in the thirteenth century

Murder most foul, as in the best it is,

But this most foul, strange, and unnatural.

GHOST OF HAMLET'S FATHER; ACT ONE, SCENE FIVE

Snowflakes twirled in the wind that moaned around the battlements. I turned up the collar of my cloak against the cold, and kept my eyes fixed on the place where the guards had told me they had seen my father's ghost.

Horatio, my oldest friend, was with me. It was Horatio who had brought me the news that my father, the king, was dead – bitten by a snake while he was sleeping in the orchard – and it was Horatio who had stood by my side at my father's funeral. Something in me died too that day, and was sealed up in the Royal Tomb with my father. My grief was so great that it sucked the light and joy out of everything.

From the courtyard below came the sound of drunken laughter.

"Someone is still celebrating the marriage of your mother and your uncle!" Horatio said.

He meant it as a joke, but the joke raised more black thoughts in my mind.

"How could she marry so soon after the funeral?" I said. "How could she forget my father so quickly?"

"You should be happy for her, my lord Hamlet," said Horatio. "She has found new happiness in the midst of sorrow, and your uncle, Claudius, will rule Denmark wisely until you come of age."

I laughed bitterly. I had seen cunning in Claudius's face, but no wisdom. I was about to say so, when midnight began to ring out from the turret above our heads.

And as the last stroke throbbed through the air, the darkness and the falling snow shaped themselves into the spirit of my father, beckoning to me.

Horatio gasped out a warning, but I paid no attention. I ran through the dancing flakes, my heart beating so fast that I thought it would burst.

The ghost was dressed in armour, a circlet of gold gleaming against the black iron of its helm. Its face was my father's face, but twisted in agony, its eyes burning like cold, blue flames. Its voice was a groan of despair that sent shudders down my backbone.

"Hamlet, my son! My spirit cannot find rest until my murder has been avenged."

"Murder?" I cried.

"The serpent who stung me in the orchard was my brother, Claudius," said the ghost. "As I lay asleep, it was he who crept to my side and poured poison in my ear. Claudius took my life, my throne and now my wife. Avenge me, Hamlet!"

Before I could say more, the ghost faded into snowy blackness, and the echoes of its voice became the whistling of the wind.

My mind reeled. Had I really spoken to the ghost of my father, or was it a devil from Hell, sent to trick me into doing evil? I had suspected that Claudius might have had something to do with my father's death, but could I trust the word of a vision from beyond the grave? How could I be sure of the truth? How could I, the Prince of Denmark, not yet twenty years' old, avenge the death of a king?

I turned, and stumbled back to Horatio. His face was grey and he quivered with fear. "Such sights are enough to drive a man mad!" he whispered.

I laughed then, long and hard, because Horatio had unwittingly provided me with an answer.

Who could have more freedom than a mad prince? If I pretended to be mad, I could say whatever I wished and search for the truth without arousing Claudius's suspicion.

✦   ✦   ✦

And so my plan took shape. I wore nothing but black. I wandered through the castle, weeping and sighing, seeking out shadowy places to brood. If anyone spoke to me, I answered with the first wild nonsense that came into my head, and all the time I watched Claudius, looking for the slightest sign of guilt. I cut myself off from all friends – except Horatio; I told him everything, for I knew he was the only one I could trust.

A rumour began to spread through the castle that grief had turned my wits. So far, my plan was a success, but it is one thing to invent a plan, and another thing to carry it through. The strain of pretending, of cutting myself off from kindness and good company, was almost too great to bear. There were times when I thought I truly had gone mad, when I felt I could no longer carry the burden of what the ghost had told me. If I avenged my father, my mother's new husband would be revealed as a murderer, and her happiness would be shattered; if I did not, my father's soul was doomed to eternal torment.

Worst of all, I was tortured by doubt. What if Claudius were innocent? What if I had been deceived by an evil spirit? Questions went spinning through my mind, like the stars spinning around the Earth.

Then one day, on a bleak afternoon, alone in my room, I drew my dagger and stared at it. The blade was sharp: if I used it on myself, death would come quickly, and all my doubts and worries would be over – but what then? Would I be sending my soul into an even worse torture? I weighed the dagger in my hand, balancing the fear of what I must do to avenge my father against the fear of what might follow death. It seemed I lacked both the courage to go on with my life, and the courage to end it.

Hearing a knock at my door, I sheathed the dagger and called out, "Come in!" almost relieved at the interruption.

A woman entered. It was Lady Ophelia, her fair hair shining like a candle-flame, her eyes filled with love and concern.

My heart lifted, then sank. Ophelia and I had loved each other since we were children. Before my father's death, I had been

certain that she was the
one I would marry – but
now everything had
changed. There was no
room in my heart for love.

"Lord Hamlet?"
Ophelia said. "My father
asks if you will attend the
performance of the Royal
Players tonight?"

As soon as she
mentioned her father, I
knew what was happening.
Her father was Polonius,
the Royal Chamberlain, a
meddling fool who loved
gossip and secrets. He had
sent Ophelia to try and
discover why I was acting

so strangely. Ophelia would report everything I said to Polonius, and he
would report it to Claudius. I was sickened: the castle of Elsinore was a
place where brothers murdered brothers, wives forgot their husbands,
and fathers used their daughters as spies.

I laughed carelessly, to hide the ache I felt when I looked at Ophelia's
beautiful face. "Tell Lord Polonius that I shall be at the play," I said.

Ophelia turned her head, and I saw a tear fall across her cheek. "My
lord," she murmured, "why do you never look at me the way you used
to? There was a time when I believed you loved me, and wished us to
marry, but now you seem so cold…"

I longed to tell her how much I loved her, and that my coldness was
nothing more than acting, but I did not dare. "*You*, marry me?" I said

roughly. "Marry no one, Ophelia! Wives and husbands are all cheats and liars. It would be better for you to join a convent and become a nun!"

At this she ran from the room, her sobs echoing through the corridor, making my heart break.

And then, just as I thought there was no end to my despair, an idea came – first a glimmer, then a gleam, then a burst of light brighter than the sun.

I hurried from my room and went to the Great Hall, where the actors were setting up their stage. I found their leader, a tall man with a look of my uncle about him. After chatting for a few moments, I said casually, "Do you know the play *The Murder of Gonzago*?"

"Certainly, my lord!" came the reply.

I handed the man a purse filled with gold. "Act it tonight," I said. "But I want you to make some changes to the story. Listen carefully…"

I meant to turn the play from an entertainment into a trap – a trap to catch a King.

+   +   +

That evening, while the audience watched the stage, I watched Claudius. At first he showed little interest in the story, preferring to whisper to my mother and kiss her fingers in a way that filled me with loathing – but gradually the skill of the players won his attention. At the end of the first scene, exactly according to my instructions, the actor playing Duke Gonzago lay down as though asleep and his nephew Lucianus – played by the actor who resembled Claudius – crept up on him and poured poison into his ear.

Even though the light in the hall was dim, I could see the deathly pallor of Claudius's face as he watched this scene. His eyes grew troubled, and he raised a trembling hand towards the stage.

I knew then that I was gazing at the face of a murderer, and that everything the ghost had told me was true.

"No!" Claudius cried out, springing to his feet. "Lights! Bring more lights!"

But all the torches in the world would not light the darkness in his mind. His nerve failed and he hurried from the hall.

Mother made to follow him, but I stopped her at the door. "Do not delay me. I must go to the King!" she said. "Something is wrong."

"And I know what," I told her. "I must talk to you. I will come to your room in an hour. Make sure you are alone, and tell no one of our meeting."

✦   ✦   ✦

But I underestimated Claudius's cunning, and the power he had over my mother. When she let me into her room, there was a coldness in her expression and I guessed that she had been speaking to my uncle. Before I could say a word, she said, "Hamlet, you have deeply offended your royal stepfather."

"And you have offended my dead father," I replied.

Mother frowned at me, puzzled. "What do you mean?" she demanded.

"You offended him the day you abandoned your mourning robes in exchange for a wedding gown," I said. "The day you married a liar and a murderer!"

"I won't listen!" Mother shouted. She began to cover her ears with her

hands and I caught hold of her wrists to prevent her – she had to hear the truth. Mother screamed in alarm, and then I heard a voice from behind the drawn curtains at her window, calling out, "Help! Murder!"

I was certain it was Claudius – who else would skulk and spy in my mother's bedroom? I drew my sword and plunged it into the curtain, filled with fierce joy that my father was avenged at last...

But it was the body of Lord Polonius that tumbled into the room; I had killed an innocent man. "You meddling old fool!" I groaned. "What were you doing there?"

"Following my orders," said a voice.

I turned and saw Claudius in the doorway, with two armed guards. A triumphant light glinted in his eyes. "I was afraid you might harm your mother if you were alone with her," Claudius went on. "Your madness has made you violent, Hamlet. You must leave Denmark tonight. I shall send you to friends in England, who will care for you until you are back in your right mind. Guards, take the Prince away!"

Neither my mother nor the guards saw the mocking smile that flickered on his lips, but as soon as I saw it, I knew that Claudius intended me never to return from England. I would be imprisoned, and then secretly murdered.

While I had been trying to trap my uncle, he had been setting a trap for me, and now it had snapped shut.

+   +   +

They bundled me into a windowless carriage and locked the doors and I was driven speedily through the night. I could see nothing, and could hear only the rattling of the wheels and the cracking of the driver's whip, keeping the horses at full gallop. After several hours, the carriage arrived at a port, and I was placed on a ship that set sail almost as soon as I was aboard. I made no attempt to escape. It was all over: my father was unavenged, Claudius had outwitted me, and I was as good as dead.

Just before dawn broke, my life seemed to become some strange dream, for the most unlikely thing happened: I was rescued by Danish pirates. They captured the ship and murdered most of the crew, but when they discovered who I was, panic seized them. Fearing that they would be hunted down by the Danish fleet, the pirates sailed back to Denmark and put me ashore at a little fishing village. There I found lodgings and wrote letters to Horatio, and to my mother. I told her that I would return to Elsinore and right all the wrongs that had been done – though I did not tell her what those wrongs were.

The next day, I bought a horse and set off, certain that Fate had returned me to Denmark to complete my revenge. There was no more doubt in my mind – Claudius was guilty, and I would make him answer for his crime.

I was still some way from the castle when I was met by Horatio, who had ridden out to find me. There was a darkness in my friend's face, and I knew he was the bearer of ill tidings.

"My lord," he said, "the Lady Ophelia is dead. Claudius told her that you had killed her father, and the grief drove her so mad that she drowned herself."

Tears blurred my sight. What had I done to my beloved Ophelia!

In another time and place, our love might have grown into happiness…

"Ophelia's brother, Laertes, has sworn to kill you for the deaths of his father and sister," Horatio went on, "but Claudius persuaded Laertes to settle his differences with you in a fencing match, in front of the whole court. I have seen the King whispering to Laertes in private, and I am sure they are plotting against you. Turn back, my lord! Escape while you can to somewhere you will be safe!"

"No, I must go to Elsinore," I told him. "My destiny awaits me there. We cannot escape our destinies, Horatio, we can only be ready for them, and I am ready."

✦   ✦   ✦

And so the ghost, Claudius, the pirates and my destiny have brought me back, to the torch-light and candles of the Great Hall at Elsinore. Courtiers and nobles chatter idly and make wagers on the outcome of the duel. There, on the royal thrones, sit my uncle and my mother. She smiles at me and looks proud; he is anxious, and keeps glancing slyly at Laertes. Laertes is filled with a cold hatred that makes his eyes shine like moonlight on ice.

Horatio takes my cloak and hands me a rapier. His face is pale and worried. He leans close and whispers, "Have a care, my lord! There is death in Laertes' look."

I smile: death is everywhere in the castle of Elsinore tonight, and I can feel my father's spirit hovering over me.

Claudius raises his right arm. "Let the contest begin!" he commands.

The blades of our rapiers snick and squeal. Our shadows, made huge and menacing by the torches, flicker on the walls as we duck and dodge. Laertes is a skilled swordsman, but rage and hate have made him clumsy. He drops his guard to strike at me, I flick my wrist, and the point of my rapier catches his arm.

One of the marshals shouts, "A hit! First hit to Prince Hamlet!"

Laertes bows, his forehead slick with sweat. "Let us take a cup of wine

and catch our breath, my lord," he says.

The wine cups are on a table near the thrones. Laertes and I step towards them, and my mother suddenly snatches up one of the cups. "A toast, to honour my beloved son!" she announces.

"No!" hisses Claudius. He reaches out as if to dash the cup from my mother's lips, but he is too late: she has drunk the wine down to the dregs.

There is just time for me to see a look of horror on Claudius's face, and then, without warning, Laertes wheels around and slashes at me with his sword. I parry the blow, realising that this is no longer a contest – I am fighting for my life.

I see Laertes' eyes, blind with fury. I watch his mouth twist itself into an ugly snarl. He clutches at me and tries to stab under my arm, but I catch the sword in my left hand and I wrench it from his grasp. A pain like fire burns against my palm, and my fingers are wet with blood.

I step back, throw Laertes my rapier and take his in my right hand. "*En garde!*" I say.

We fight on, but something is wrong. Laertes looks terrified, and his breath comes in sobs. The pain in my hand is fierce, throbbing up into my forearm – I have suffered from sword-cuts before, but none as painful as this.

Laertes lunges desperately at me, and the point of my sword scratches through his shirt; a spurt of red stains the whiteness of the linen.

Laertes reels back. "We are dead men!" he groans. "The King spread poison on the blade – the same poison that he poured into your wine cup!"

I see all now. I understand the hot agony that is creeping through my left arm and across my chest.

Laertes cries out, "The King is a murderer!" and crumples to the floor. At the same time, my mother screams and topples from her throne.

There is no time left. I must act quickly, before the pain reaches my heart. I stagger towards Claudius and he cringes in his throne, covering his face with his hands.

"Traitor!" I say, and drive the poisoned sword deep into his heart.

Voices shout...people are running. I fall back, and someone catches me. I think it is Horatio, but I cannot see him clearly, for a darkness is falling before my eyes...coming down like the snow falling, that night on the battlements...

Through the darkness, I seem to see a light...and my father's face... and everything drops away behind me...

Horatio's voice whispers, "Farewell, sweet Prince!

And the rest is silence.

There's a divinity that shapes our ends,
Rough-hew them how we will.
HAMLET: ACT FIVE, SCENE TWO

THE TEMPEST

How magic helps to right an old wrong

CAST LIST

PROSPERO a wizard, the rightful Duke of Milan

MIRANDA daughter to Prospero

CALIBAN servant to Prospero

ARIEL an airy spirit

PRINCE FERDINAND son to the King of Naples

TRINCULO AND STEPHANO sailors

ALONSO King of Naples

ANTONIO, DUKE OF MILAN brother to Prospero

THE SCENE
Mediterranean island
in the fifteenth century

O, I have suffered
With those that I saw suffer! A brave vessel,
Who had, no doubt, some noble creature in her,
Dashed all to pieces!

MIRANDA; ACT ONE, SCENE THREE

A violent storm was raging over the island. Palm trees bent and swayed like dancers in the howling gale that tore off their branches and sent them tumbling through the air.

On a beach not far from the mouth of his cave, stood Prospero the wizard, his white hair and beard streaming out in the wind, his black robes flapping around him. As he raised his left hand, thunder rumbled; he lifted the staff in his right hand, and forked lightning crackled, flickering like snakes' tongues across the inky clouds.

Out to sea, a ship with broken masts and tattered sails wallowed helplessly as the storm drove it towards a jagged coral-reef.

A lovely young woman in a white gown hurried out of the cave and ran towards Prospero, her dark hair whipping about her face. She caught the wizard by the sleeve and called out, "Father!"

Prospero seemed not to hear her. His eyes burned silver with magic, and they stayed firmly fixed on the ship.

"Father!" shouted the young woman. "What are you doing? Everyone aboard that ship will be killed!"

Above the sound of the wind came a groaning crash of timber striking rock. A huge wave reared up like a startled horse and thundered down on the ship, making it vanish from sight.

Prospero lowered his hands. The wind dropped to a gentle breeze, the boiling clouds faded into a blue sky and the sun glinted on a calm sea.

"No one has been harmed, Miranda," said Prospero. "Everything is as I planned. For your sake, I have used my magic to help right a great wrong, done long ago."

"What wrong, Father?" Miranda asked with a puzzled frown.

"Enough!" said Prospero. He moved his left hand in front of Miranda's face, and she fell into an enchanted sleep where she stood.

Prospero took two paces towards the sea, looking out at the place where the ship had sunk. "Soon, my brother!" he whispered.

A sound made him turn his head in time to see a strange creature creeping up behind Miranda. It was shaped like a man, but its skin was covered with glistening green scales, and its eyes were as yellow as a lizard's.

"Caliban!" Prospero said sternly. "You brought no wood or water to the cave this morning. Must I send the spirits to torment you again?"

Caliban scowled. "I was not born to be your servant!" he answered defiantly. "My mother, the great witch Sycorax, promised me that I would rule this island, and so I would have – if you had not come here, and stolen her books of magic, and freed her slave-spirits to help you drive her away!"

"Silence!" said Prospero, and he snapped his fingers.

Needles of fire seemed to lance through Caliban, forcing him to his knees. "Mercy, master, mercy!" he cried, bowing his head. The pain left him, and he hid his face so that Prospero could not see his cunning smile. "Why are you so cruel?" he whimpered. "You were kind to me once!"

"And you repaid my kindness by trying to kidnap my daughter!"

snapped Prospero. "Get to work, you treacherous wretch!"

Caliban stood, and shambled off. "I will be revenged, one day!" he muttered to himself. "I will be King of this island, and I will take Miranda as my Queen!"

When Caliban was safely out of sight, Prospero lifted his staff. "Ariel!" he called softly. "Appear to me now, sweet spirit!"

There was a faint sound of music. Lights sparkled in the air, winking like sunshine on bursting bubbles. In the midst of the lights fluttered a young boy, with golden skin and white wings on his heels. He smiled at Prospero, and darted playfully around his head.

Prospero laughed. "Faithful Ariel!" he said. "Are the sailors scattered over the island as I commanded?"

"They are, good master," said Ariel, his voice like the gentle humming of a harp.

"And where is Ferdinand, the King of Naples' son?" Prospero demanded.

"Close by," said Ariel. "He mourns his father, believing him to be drowned."

"He is not drowned," said Prospero. "He wanders the island lost, with my brother Antonio." Prospero sighed, and old memories gave his face a far off look. "Twelve years ago, when I was Duke of Milan, my wife died," he said sadly. "Grief blinded me to the treachery of Antonio, who plotted in secret with my old enemy, King Alonso of Naples. They overthrew me, and Antonio took my place. I was put in an open boat with my daughter, and cast adrift to die. But destiny took me to this island, to Sycorax's magic books, and you. My spells brought the ship here, and now it is time for mischief and magic."

"And revenge, master?" said Ariel.

Prospero shook his head. "I do not seek revenge, only justice," he said. "Go to Prince Ferdinand and bring him here!"

Ariel's eyes darkened into doubt. "Will it be as thou promised,

master? When thy plan is done, shall I be free?"

"Free as the wind, my Ariel," said Prospero. "I will break my spells, and no magic will ever hold you again."

Ariel glowed brightly, and flew off faster than Prospero's eyes could follow.

+   +   +

Prince Ferdinand was seated cross-legged on the sand. Salt water and the sun had bleached his brown hair almost blond, and his handsome face was lined with sadness. Whenever he closed his eyes, he saw the massive waves that had swallowed the ship and cast him up on this uncharted island. He might never be found, and he wondered if it would be better to swim out to sea and join his drowned father than face a life of miserable loneliness...

His thoughts were suddenly interrupted by lights dancing in front of his face, swarming like bees. They were so fascinating that Ferdinand could do nothing but stare at them. Then he heard music, and the singing of a sweet, high voice.

"Forget thy father, deep he lies,
With shining pearls set in his eyes.
Come with me now, Prince Ferdinand
And walk along the yellow sand!"

Ferdinand seemed to be caught up in a dream. Without a word he stood, and followed where the lights led him.

+   +   +

Prospero saw Ferdinand from afar, following bewitched behind Ariel's glimmering lights. When the young Prince was close by, Prospero touched Miranda on the shoulder, releasing her from the spell. Instantly, she woke, and the first thing she saw was Ferdinand. "Is this a spirit, Father?" she gasped.

"No, my child. It is a man of flesh and blood like you and me," Prospero told her.

"But I thought all men had white hair and beards, like yours!" Miranda exclaimed.

Prospero smiled, and signalled to Ariel. The dancing lights vanished, and Ferdinand's trance was broken. He saw Miranda, and his eyes filled with wonder at her beauty. "Am I still dreaming?" he whispered. "Is this a vision?"

"I am no vision, sir," Miranda said. "I am as real as you are…if you are indeed real." Shyly, she reached out her hand. Ferdinand reached out his, and their fingertips touched.

"I saw in the stars that you were meant for each other," Prospero said softly. "Your love will undo all the evil done by hatred."

Miranda and Ferdinand heard nothing of this, for they were totally lost in each other.

"Ariel!" said Prospero. "Find King Alonso and my brother Antonio, and when you do…"

Ariel listened carefully, and before long the air was bright with his laughter.

+   +   +

On another part of the beach, two sailors swayed across the sand, leaning against each other to stop themselves from falling over. One was Trinculo, a thin man with ginger hair and a freckled face, and his companion was Stephano, who had a shock of grey hair and a stomach as round as a watermelon. They had been washed ashore together with a cask of wine, which they had fast consumed. Now they were so drunk, that when Caliban jumped out from behind a rock and grovelled at their feet, they were not entirely sure that he was really there.

Caliban had been watching Trinculo and Stephano for some time, and his quick, cunning mind had seen a way to use them to get rid of his master, Prospero.

"Gentle Gods!" Caliban cried. "Have you come from the sky to save me?"

"He thinks we're Gods!" Trinculo giggled.

"Hmm, he's an ugly brute, but he knows good breeding when he sees it!" whispered Stephano. "That's right, we're Gods from the moon," he said to Caliban.

"Save me!" Caliban begged. "Save me from the wicked enchanter who has enslaved me, and I will give you all his treasure and be your faithful servant forever!"

"Enchanter?" yelped Trinculo, turning pale.

"Courage, Trinculo!" Stephano murmured. "And what kind of treasure might that be, good monster?"

"Gold," said Caliban. "And silver. And many jewels."

Stephano drew his cutlass and waved it so clumsily that he almost cut off his right ear. "Pirates, enchanters – it's all the same to me!" he boasted. "Take me to the villain! I'll carve him into thin slices!"

With a whoop of delight, Caliban led the way along the jungle track to Prospero's cave.

After the long walk through the jungle's heat, and shadows, and strange sounds, Stephano's head began to clear and he no longer felt as bold as he had earlier, and Trinculo was trembling like a mouse's whiskers.

"Er, is it much further?" Stephano asked Caliban.

"There!" Caliban replied, pointing.

Trinculo stood on tiptoes and peered. He could see the mouth of a cave, filled with an ominous darkness.

"Why d-don't we walk s-side by s-side?" he jibbered. "Then n-nothing can harm us!"

Even as he spoke, the darkness in the cave began to move. It poured out of the cave-mouth, coiling like black mist – and the mist transformed itself into a pack of savage black dogs, with red eyes and slavering fangs. Snapping and snarling, the dogs bounded towards the intruders.

Trinculo and Stephano turned and ran screaming into the jungle, with Caliban close behind.

✦   ✦   ✦

King Alonso and Antonio had also been wandering through the jungle for hours, and now they were desperate with thirst and hunger. Their fine clothes, ripped by cruel thorns, hung round them in tatters, and sweat streamed down their faces. Alonso, certain that Ferdinand was dead, was stricken with grief, and at last he slumped on to the trunk of a fallen tree.

"I can go no further!" he groaned. "I will wait here for death to put an end to my misery!"

Antonio glanced around uneasily. The jungle was an eerie place, full of shadows and whispering voices. "Just a little further, my lord!" he said. "I see a clearing not far ahead. Perhaps we will find a spring of fresh water there." The thought of water urged Alonso to his feet and together the two men stumbled towards the edge of the clearing.

Like a mirage, in the middle of the clearing stood a long table, piled with food and drink – golden platters of carved meats, whole roasted fowl, baskets of bread and golden jugs of wine.

Alonso and Antonio hurried towards it, but before they could reach the feast, there was a dazzling flash of light and Ariel appeared. He hovered over the table in the shape of a harpy – a monster with a human head and the body of a gigantic eagle. Alonso tried to snatch a jug of wine, but the harpy hissed and slashed at him with its bronze talons.

"Foul spirit, why do you torment us?" Antonio sobbed.

"For thy betrayal of thy brother Prospero and niece Miranda!" the harpy screeched. "Thou and King Alonso did set them in a boat and leave them to the mercy of the ocean. Prepare thee for thy punishment!"

Alonso and Antonio stared in amazement, wondering how the spirit had discovered their guilty secret. They expected the harpy to tear them into pieces, but instead it faded into a cloud of tiny lights that swirled like specks of dust floating in a beam of sunlight. The two men felt themselves fall into a waking sleep, and heard a voice speaking to them out of the cloud. "Come!" it said. "Follow, follow!"

+   +   +

From all over the island, the crew of the wrecked ship came to gather on the beach near Prospero's cave, drawn there by magic – even Trinculo and Stephano, who had aching heads and torn clothes from where the hounds had snapped at them. The sailors rejoiced to see friends they thought had perished, and gazed about in wonder. Had the storm only been a dream, or were they dreaming now? For there was their ship, undamaged, anchored close to the shore. The sailors laughed, and scratched their heads, unable to believe their luck.

Ariel brought Alonso and Antonio to the mouth of Prospero's cave, and broke their trance. Alonso gasped as Ferdinand and Miranda stepped

out of the darkness, hand in hand, and his eyes blurred with tears. "What wonderful new world is this that has such people in it?" he wondered.

"The world that will be made when we return to Naples and our children are joined in marriage," said a voice.

Alonso and Antonio turned, and saw Prospero standing behind them. Antonio could not meet his brother's eyes, and hung his head in shame.

"Let our old hate be ended by their young love, Alonso," Prospero said. He came forward, and placed his hand on Antonio's shoulder. "I forgive you, brother," he said. "We will rule Milan together and end our days in peace. Now, go down to the shore and make ready to leave this island forever."

"Are you coming, Father?" asked Miranda.

"In a moment, my child," Prospero said. He waited until he was alone, then whispered, "Ariel?"

Ariel grew out of emptiness. Too excited to hold one shape, he turned into a humming bird, then a butterfly, then a winged unicorn.

"I have burned my books of magic and my wizard's staff," Prospero declared. "You are free to go, my Ariel, but I shall sadly miss you!"

"And I shall miss thee, dear master!" said Ariel. "But look for me in springtime blossom, or when the summer breeze stirs thy curtain, or when the winter stars blaze bright. Until then, farewell!"

"Farewell, sweet spirit!" said Prospero, and he turned away so that Ariel would not see the tears in his eyes.

+   +   +

As the ship's sails unfurled and it began to glide away, Caliban came out of his hiding place in the jungle. He danced on the beach, turning cartwheels as he whooped, "I am King of the island! King!"

His voice frightened a flock of parrots who clattered out of the treetops and flew over Caliban in a great circle, their plumage glittering like the jewels in a royal crown.

Our revels now are ended. These our actors,
As I foretold you, were all spirits, and
Are melted into air, into thin air:
PROSPERO: ACT FOUR, SCENE ONE

SHAKESPEARE AND THE GLOBE

Some of Shakespeare's most famous plays were first performed at the Globe Theatre, where he worked as a playwright and a minor performer. The Globe was built on the south bank of the River Thames in 1599. At that time London was growing fast. It was a dirty, bustling city of lords and ladies, rich merchants, shopkeepers, sailors, beggars, pickpockets and cut-throats – an exciting and dangerous place. Most Londoners worked hard to make a living and in their precious free time they liked to be entertained. They danced, drank and gambled in taverns, went to see bear-baiting, bull-baiting, cock-fighting – and plays.

Originally, plays were put on by groups of actors who toured the city, performing wherever they could, most often in the courtyards of inns, some of which had permanent stages erected. London's first playhouse, the Theatre, was built in 1576 on a road that ran northwards out of the city – a good place to attract an audience. For many years, the Theatre was popular and successful, but there was an argument between James Burbage, the manager, and his landlord, Giles Allen. The Theatre closed down in 1597 and timbers from the demolished building were used to make the framework of the Globe.

Going to the Globe was a different experience from going to the theatre today. The building was roughly circular in shape, but with flat sides: a little like a doughnut crossed with a fifty-pence piece. The ring of the doughnut was roofed with reed thatch; the hole in the middle was open to the sky. Because the Globe was an open-air theatre, plays were only put on during daylight hours in spring and summer. People paid a penny to stand in the central space and watch a play, and this part of the audience became known as 'the groundlings' because they stood on the ground. A place in the tiers of seating beneath the thatched roof, where there was a slightly better view and less chance of being rained on, cost extra.

The Elizabethans did not bath very often and the audiences at the Globe were smelly. Fine ladies and gentlemen in the more expensive seats sniffed perfume and

bags of sweetly-scented herbs to cover the stink rising from the groundlings.

Audiences were not well-behaved. They would cheer the heroes and heroines, and boo and hiss the villains, rather like a modern pantomime audience. People clapped and cheered when their favourite actors came on stage; bad actors were jeered at and sometimes pelted with whatever came to hand. If the audience considered any part of the play to be boring, they would ignore it and chatter among themselves as they munched on the apples and hazelnuts they had bought on the way in.

On the stage, too, things were different. There were no actresses: all the female characters in Shakespeare's plays would have been acted by boys, wearing wigs and make-up. So in *Twelfth Night*, when Viola dresses up as Cesario to find a place at Count Orsino's court, the audience would have seen a boy pretending to be a girl who was pretending to be a boy.

Costumes were made from the finest materials, wigs and beards were made from dyed horse-hair and looked astonishingly real. A lot of attention was paid to special effects: witches and demons sprang up from trap doors, gods and goddesses were lowered on ropes and pulleys from the roof over the stage. Smoke, made by lighting small heaps of gunpowder, rolled across the battle-scenes. Sheets of copper were rattled to imitate the sound of thunder, and the noise of a howling wind came from a wooden drum being turned inside a roll of canvas. To make sword-fights seem more realistic, pigs' bladders filled with blood from butchers' shops were hidden in the actors' costumes, and pierced with the point of a sword or dagger.

In 1613, during a performance of Shakespeare's play *King Henry the Eighth*, the special effects caused a disaster. A stage cannon was let off, and burning wadding from it stuck in the thatch of the roofing, setting it alight. The audience of almost three thousand people escaped unhurt, except for one poor man whose breeches caught fire. Luckily, he was able to put out the flames with a bottle of ale; but the Globe was not so lucky, it was completely destroyed.

Money was raised to build a second Globe on the remains of the first, and Shakespeare, who was wealthy and famous by this time, became a part-owner of the new building. It continued in use until 1642, when all the London theatres were

closed because of the Civil War. It was finally pulled down in 1644.

Unfortunately for modern scholars, the few surviving pictures of the Globe that were drawn while it was still standing, only showed its outside, and even its exact location was unclear, but because of the theatre's connection with Shakespeare, its name was never forgotten.

In the United States, where over a hundred Shakespeare festivals are held each year, several theatres were named after the Globe, the most famous being in Oregon and Utah. In 1959, the Oregon Shakespeare Festival built an Elizabethan Theatre, where at last Shakespeare's plays could be performed in the open to give audiences some idea of how they might have looked and sounded when they were first acted.

Britain had to wait longer for its Globe. In 1970, the American actor, Sam Wannamaker, founded the Shakespeare Globe Playhouse Trust. His dream was to build a replica of Shakespeare's Globe making it as close to the original as possible and placing it near the original site. Building began in 1987 from plans based on Elizabethan drawings of other London theatres. Two years later, the remains of part of the original Globe's foundations were found. Archaeologists were able to discover more about its construction, and they passed the information on to the builders of the new theatre. The reconstructed Globe opened for its first season in 1997. Sadly, Sam Wannamaker died before the work was completed.

So once more there is a Globe Theatre on the south bank of the Thames. It is made from the same materials that the Elizabethan builders would have used – wood, plaster and thatch. Groundlings have to stand in the open, come rain or shine (umbrellas are not allowed) but it is to be hoped they are better-behaved and not as smelly as the groundlings that Shakespeare would have known. The rest of the audience sit under cover on wooden benches.

This is as close as we can come to the theatre where Shakespeare first created his magic. It stands as a tribute to Britain's greatest playwright, and to Sam Wannamaker, a man who worked so hard to make his dream come true, and then left it for us to share.

ANGELA BARRETT WRITES ABOUT THE ILLUSTRATIONS

I have always wanted to illustrate a collection of stories from Shakespeare – what a gift for any illustrator! As the stories are based on plays the possibility of giving the characters one's own interpretation of their personalities is endless. So, for example, Hamlet is dressed in black clothing to signify his distress, but I have given him dirty hair too, showing that he had really let himself go. And Ophelia wears white as a symbol of her purity. In *Twelfth Night* Malvolio's comic obedience to Olivia gives enormous scope for creating a character full of mockery!

All the plays in this collection take place in periods which particularly appeal to me for their vividness of costume and sheer grandeur of setting. The costumes, weapons, armour and furniture for all the stories were researched from paintings of the same period, from history, architecture and costume books. I have tried to be accurate, but sometimes I have had to guess or have invented because I wanted the colours to suit the mood of a scene and the characters.

Every artist brings their own individual viewpoint and interpretation to the illustration of classic stories. Here is just a little of the background to my approach in capturing the variety of moods and changing emotions which create the fascination of Shakespeare's theatre.

✦

A MIDSUMMER NIGHT'S DREAM

This play has been illustrated by many artists, and I have tried to keep my interpretation as individual as possible.

I have only ever had one idea of what fairies look like, and see them as insect-like creatures, with no specific clothes but wrapped in gossamer or cocoon-like material, not of this world, holding magical powers.

I love shoes, which is why I chose to show the feet of the lovers running in the forest. There was an enormous variety of beautiful sandals in Greece at the time, so I

have picked out a few that I liked and worked around these to make the designs interesting. In fact, the costumes and hairstyles of the human characters are all based on styles found on vase paintings from ancient Greece.

✦

KING HENRY THE FIFTH

This play presented a wonderful opportunity to address the heroic beauty of this period of history. Many of the illustrations in this story are based on references which I found in medieval manuscripts, from the armour worn by the soldiers to the tapestry hanging behind King Henry as he sits on his throne. I painted the roses in the tapestry red and white as signifiers of the Wars of the Roses, a series of civil wars begun in the reign of Henry VI, Henry V's son.

The trees in the scene that takes place before the battle are based on some woodland photos I have from a holiday in France. I made them tall and wintry to give the feeling of bleakness and a sense of loss: the soldiers had already lost many of their friends in battle and would have been terrified that they too might die the next day. For this reason I didn't paint any bright or splendid battle tents which I like very much but which seemed to detract from the grimness of war.

✦

ROMEO AND JULIET

Juliet's mask is drawn from one I bought in Venice, although mine is covered in deep yellow damask. I think it would have been more accurate to give her a black mask, but I like this one, and it links with the little white cat in the background of the balcony scene. Her ball dress is copied from a painting by Ghirlandaio of 1488. It is the only costume in the book which I have copied so closely.

Juliet's garden is loosely based on the garden at the Villa Rufulo in Ravello, which is much further south than Verona, and the vault in which Juliet is buried is taken from aspects of various Italian paintings. Like the chapel (which is entirely fictitious), it is very plain; I felt that the chapel would only be a small place of worship, and therefore wouldn't be too decorative.

I have tried to bring out the oppressive heat of the sun and the cold feel of the stone

in the painting of the fountain, which is based on the fountain at Riva, a town on Lake Garda in northern Italy.

The colours of the clothes of Romeo and Juliet are young, light and romantic but the settings are mostly dark or sad as befits their story.

✦

MACBETH

The colours of the costumes in *Macbeth* are taken from the Scottish landscape, which give the characters a windswept feel, echoing their cold emotions.

The illustration of the three witches when Macbeth first sees them was great fun to draw! I have always found the notion of levitation to be quite spooky, so I felt that the witches would probably be floating. To make it extra creepy I chose to paint the moment where they are seen in the flash of lightning, so the background has a lot of brilliant violet in it to try and capture this fleeting brightness.

The castle is very labyrinthine, which helps to convey the idea that Lady Macbeth is lost; she doesn't know where she's going and is overcome with guilt at what she and her husband have done. The ground is strewn with rushes (used on floors for hundreds of years) which her skirt would pick up, making a trail behind her. The corridors had to be lit for Lady Macbeth to see where she was going but I didn't want the torchlight to look too cosy, so I painted it white reversing the usual warm effect of light, making it look cold and comfortless.

✦

ANTONY AND CLEOPATRA

Many artists have painted their versions of Cleopatra's barge. For mine I have drawn on early nineteenth century engravings of Egyptian and Roman warships and traders, and these were based on ancient wall paintings and coins. The illustration of the ships at sea is drawn in the distance giving an idea of how the ships would have looked as part of a battle fleet.

This was a wonderful story to illustrate because I was able to emphasise the heat and colour of exotic Egypt. Cleopatra is a dramatic heroine, and I made her jewellery and clothing wonderfully sumptuous, basing them on ancient Egyptian tomb paintings.

Cleopatra's tomb is based on the Sphinx, a huge stone monument with the head of a Pharaoh and body of a lion. Here you can just see the toes.

✦

TWELFTH NIGHT

Olivia's garden is based on real gardens of the period, even down to the peacocks. It has a wonderfully Mediterranean feel, and I have tried to make both the plants and the architecture typical of fifteenth century life.

When Olivia sees Malvolio in his ridiculous cross-gartered stockings the little dog provides a lovely silent commentary on the humour of this scene! I felt that Malvolio was experiencing a sort of mid-life crisis, and thought that he would probably go the whole way in succumbing to what he believes to be Olivia's fashion dictates. Because of this, I have given him yellow garters and shoes, too!

Sir Toby Belch and Andrew Aguecheek are wearing colourful and ludicrous fifteenth century hats in colours which seemed to me to suit their characters. The same hats in dark colours can look quite sinister. Olivia would probably have had some sort of elaborate head-dress – but I thought she would look better without it, and with her hair loose. Viola as Cesario is wearing some rather tight riding boots, though she doesn't have a horse, but I thought she might have put them on to help her disguise and make her feel more masculine. Her head-dress is similar to Sir Toby Belch's in that it consists of a hat with a long piece of fabric to entwine around the head for decoration. However, Viola wears hers more conservatively!

The green baize under the picture of Toby Belch and Andrew Aguecheek comes from a picture of a library from this period. The furniture was covered in this material and decorated with brass and metal fittings.

✦

HAMLET

The castle at Elsinore is loosely based on Framlingham Castle in Suffolk. Although I have made some dramatic architectural alterations this was the picture that I had in my mind when I was painting it.

The painting of Queen Gertrude lifting the chalice to drink from was a particularly

hard picture to paint. I ended up painting my own hand, using a lot of mirrors to try and capture it accurately! I have made the chalice very ornate as befits a queen.

The scene in which Hamlet is talking to his mother takes place in front of a tapestry. The design on this is made up from patterns I found on clothes typical of the period.

The scene of Hamlet's death was drawn from my experience of seeing the play on different occasions. I was thinking of a very big deep stage with Hamlet and Horatio at the centre of it.

✦

THE TEMPEST

The clothes worn by Miranda and Prospero are loosely based on paintings of the period. They had been on the island a long time and their clothes are very worn. Miranda would have outgrown the clothes she was shipwrecked in and would have had to make herself some garments from rags that had come ashore from wrecked ships. She has decorated her tattered dress with shells and Caliban has made a necklace from shells and seaweed.

I particularly wanted to give the seashore scenes that wonderfully windswept and clear air feel you get immediately following a storm.

The jungle creatures are all based on real animals with a little influence from paintings by Gauguin. I have brought them all together in the forest. And I have given Trinculo and Stephano bright red faces as they had been drinking far too much alcohol and getting very hot following Caliban through the jungle.

✦   ✦   ✦

Thus far with rough and all-unable pen
Our bending author hath persued the story,
In little room confining mighty men,
Mangling by starts the full course of their glory.
CHORUS: EPILOGUE
KING HENRY THE FIFTH

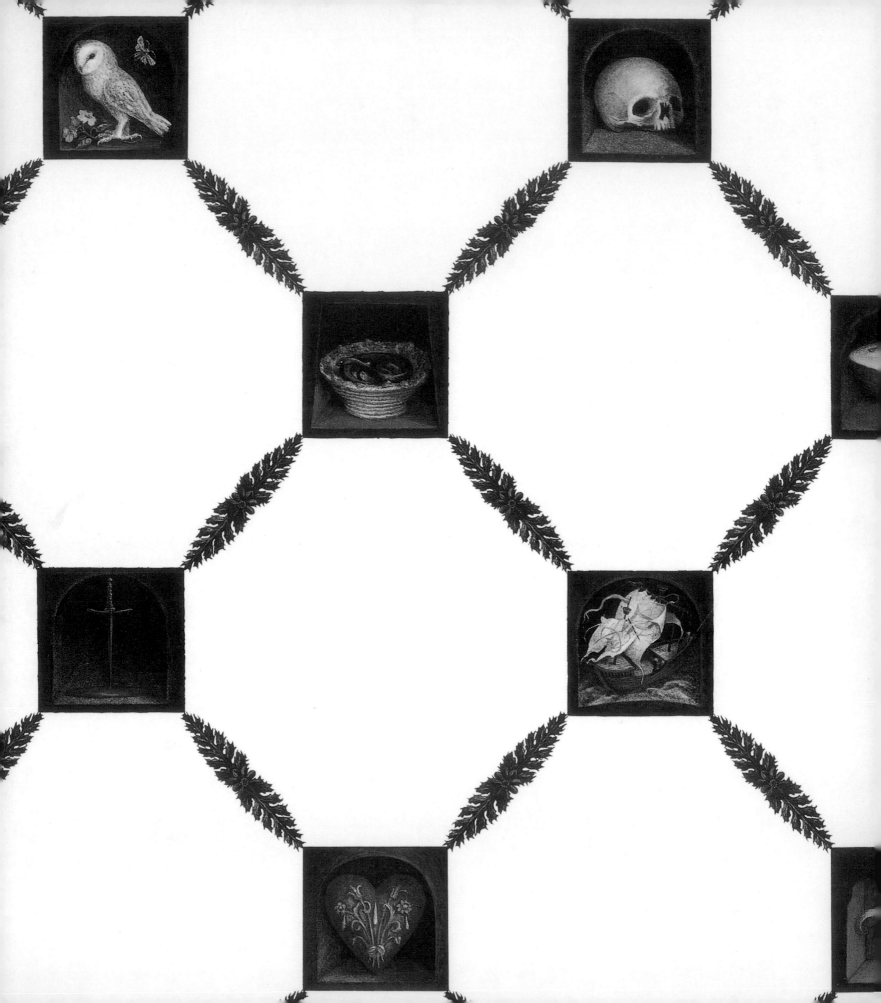